OF FLAME AND PROMISE

CECY ROBSON

OF FLAME AND PROMISE REVIEWS

"Of Flame and Promise" is an Absolutely Amazing book. I laughed, I cried, I felt their pain. It's one of the best books I have read. While this was my first book by Cecy it won't be my last. **--Night Owl Reviews (Top Pick, 5 Stars!)**

"Of Flame and Promise delivered a scorching hot romance, with humor and suspense. It was the perfect book to begin the New Year. Now I have to wait patiently for the next book!" **--Caffeinated Book Reviewer**

"The only bad thing is that Cecy can't write this series fast enough for me. I want more and I want it now!" **--Addicted to Happily Ever After**

"So, looking forward to what comes next in this exciting, passionate, gritty series that I heartily recommend to Paranormal Romance and Urban Fantasy fans, alike." **--Delighted Reader**

"The Weird Girls is one of my favorite series. One that I look forward to read, and as usual with Mrs. Cecy Robson, this is a book to read

when you have the time, because you are going to lie to yourself, by believing that it will be one more chapter and you will go to bed. It will not happen, so either make sure you have the time or you'll be happy you didn't sleep, because you will keep on thinking about the book during the day." **--The Bookaholic Cat**

"[Of Flame and Promise] was everything, everything I was hoping it would be. Cecy once again astounds in her ability to make me love and make me feel with the stroke of her pen.
" **--My Guilty Obsession**

"Of Flame and Promise was exciting, funny, and oh la la sexy! I can't wait to get more of Taran and Gemini." **--Christys Love of Books**

"Of Flame and Promise was a splendid read. It gives us an entertaining plot, danger, action, romance, snark, and a couple I have been waiting to read more about. If you are a fan of the Weird Girls series, you don't want to miss out on picking up this novella." **-- Angel's Guilty Pleasures**

"Oh my goodness- this book is slap your momma good! It has it all: action packed, passion filled and of course sisterly love. The kind that slaps you in the face with truth and protects you like a momma bear from all other harm." **--The Reading Cave**

TITLES BY CECY ROBSON

The Weird Girls Series

Gone Hunting
A Curse Awakened: A Novella
The Weird Girls: A Novella
Sealed with a Curse
A Cursed Embrace
Of Flame and Promise
A Cursed Moon: A Novella
Cursed by Destiny
A Cursed Bloodline
A Curse Unbroken
Of Flame and Light
Of Flame and Fate
Of Flame and Fury (coming soon)

The Shattered Past Series

Once Perfect
Once Loved

Once Pure

The O'Brien Family Novels

Once Kissed
Let Me
Crave Me
Feel Me
Save Me

The Carolina Beach Novels

Inseverable
Eternal
Infinite

In Too Far Novels
Salvatore

APPS
Now on *Crazy Maple's Chapters: Interactive Stories APP:* The Shattered Past and Weird Girls Series
Radish Fiction APP: Union of Souls
Also find Cecy on *Hooked – Chat stories APP* writing as Rosalina San Tiago

of Flame and Promise

A WEIRD GIRLS NOVEL

CECY ROBSON

DEDICATION

To my Weird Girls fans who stood by Celia and who now stand by Taran.

ACKNOWLEDGMENTS

To my agent, Nicole Resciniti, who believes in and nurtures my ideas—however scattered, however crazy—all the while offering her support and friendship, and yeah, sometimes a glass of wine.

To my husband, Jamie, who always takes Nic's side because, "Hey, that's a great idea!"

To Marcelino Morales: Rebecca and Claudine called you "Daddy", Douglas and I called you, "Tío", all of us knew your love.

1

———

’d woken only about an hour ago, Gemini’s warm, naked body curled against mine firing a need that required some serious quenching. So, I buried my face in his lap to stir him from sleep.

Most women would have just said good morning or nudged their partners ever so lovingly.

But I wasn’t most women.

Yeah, and you’re welcome, baby.

Gemini slowed his deep thrusts, grunting hard as he finished, his face scrunched in what appeared to be pain. But that wasn’t pain, was it? Nope, not at all. He was simply reacting to how good it felt to join his body with mine. I nibbled my way along his neck, leaving marks that faded from one bite to the next until I reached his earlobe and tugged. “Mornin’, sexy,” I whispered.

He growled something I didn’t quite understand. I didn’t speak a word of wolf, yet that deep snarl was as good as the dirty talk we’d exchanged during sex.

I laughed. Okay, maybe it wasn’t as good as those naughty

words. Yet a growl from a werewolf in his human form was a rare kind of hot few women would know.

I continued to straddle Gemini as he effortlessly carried us from the center of the room, where we'd made love standing up, and back to our bed. The gentle way in which he kissed me was in direct contrast to our wicked sex, and to the male most saw.

My lover was the second in command of the Tahoe region's Squaw Valley Den Pack—intelligent, fierce, capable of crushing skulls, quietly confident, and with fighting skills few *weres* possessed.

Not to mention he was hotter than the power I generated with my magic.

All large anatomical parts and good looks aside, Gemini was . . . kind. When you trash-talked and entered a room like you owned it like I did, it attracted a certain caliber of men. The kind that made me grateful I could protect myself with fire and lightning.

Men could be cruel, and dangerous. I knew that better than most. Unlike those men I've known in my past, I trusted Gemini.

And let's say I had trust issues.

He spread me along our tangled mess of sheets, pulling out slowly. I continued to tremble from the effects of our lovemaking, but his withdrawal made me arch my neck and groan.

His fingers brushed against my face, until I relaxed and lolled my head where he rested beside me. Dark, almond-shaped eyes stared back at me with worry. Being as lethal as he was, he could kill me without trying. But he'd never harmed me, and never would.

"Did I hurt you, Taran?" he asked quietly.

"No." I pushed up on my side and traced my finger along the edges of his neat goatee. "You know I like what you do to me." I smiled. *And you know you mean the world to me.* I glanced upward as is if thinking. "I also have the feeling you like what I do to you, too."

The fingertips of his large hand skimmed down my throat to circle my heavy breasts. I followed his stare. Light pink marks where he'd sucked and nibbled were scattered along my chest and belly, creating a path down to where his mouth had reached its intended destination. "I'm serious, Taran," he said. "I know things tend to get out of hand when we touch."

"Touch?" I mused. "Hmmm, that wasn't what you called it when we were up against the wall, or on the bed, or when you bent me over the dresser."

He laughed when I did, his hand lowering to cup my ass. Around even his closest friends, Gemini tended to be more reserved and was careful to censor his remarks. Me? Not so much. I often said what I thought, even though it always wasn't the right thing to say. My mouth notoriously got me in trouble, and frequently my actions did, too. I swear my heart was always in the right place.

Usually.

Probably.

Well, at least it was then.

"I love you, Tomo," I told him, edging closer.

His expression, so filled with lust moments before, softened. He liked it when I called him by his real name, although I did so only when we were alone and horizontal. "I love you, too," he murmured.

Tomo Hamamatsu always went by "Gemini" among his pack mates. His exceptional ability to split into two wolves earned him the nickname that made him feel accepted by his kind. I couldn't blame him for wanting to fit in—God knew it was a trick my sisters and I had never managed.

I curled against him when he pulled me closer, relishing the warmth and safety his presence always provided. I'd spent most of my life being afraid, but with Gemini beside me, I felt like nothing could hurt me. He was my everything, which was why I was so afraid to lose him.

Our time together had been limited since the start of the supernatural war. The Tribe, *were* and vamp outcasts led by demons, had all but annihilated his race.

Weres, as the earth's guardians, were held in high esteem by the witches, who were quick to form the Alliance with them. The vamps soon followed, mostly to save their own asses since they realized the Tribe would target them next. Vamps, let me say, were a whole new breed of selfish.

Gemini's hands swept down my back, comforting me when I clutched him tighter. He likely scented my fear, but I couldn't suppress it the more I thought about this hideous war. Every time he left me to go on some mission, I fell apart, terrified he wouldn't return. Many Alliance members didn't come back, like, ever—the danger factor being the reason I was frequently left to wait, stress, and swear, despite all the mojo searing its way through me.

While I looked human, I wasn't really. No mere human could wield flame and lightning from her hands or receive glimpses of the future like I could. My power made me badass. But badass didn't equate to invincible, and it sure didn't make me immortal or immune to pain.

Saving the world sucked serious donkey balls; I'd said it before, and I'll say it again. But when it came to Gemini, I was willing to risk life and limb on these suicidal missions if it meant ensuring his survival. My sexy beast wasn't willing to let me take that risk, and he flat-out refused my help. Late yesterday afternoon, I'd flung myself into his arms when he walked through the door.

I kissed his skin, right at his sternum, remembering how my tears sprouted when I saw him return. This was the first time he hadn't called to let me know he was safe. "None of the *weres* were left with phones," was what he'd said. But he wouldn't tell me how or why. Maybe I didn't want to know. It was bad enough he told me they'd lost two more members of their pack.

Gentle nibbles trailed over my shoulder, stopping along the sweep of my neck. "I'm not leaving you," he assured me quietly.

His words gave me pause. Yup. He'd scented my fear all right. "I wish I could believe you," I told him.

I didn't like sounding so pathetic. I didn't like needing someone so much. But when it came to Gemini, I couldn't help it. No matter how hard I fought that weakness.

Physically, I could give myself completely over—surrender to his muscular body, give in to those hard thrusts, and grow hotter with each hair pull. The physical was easy for me. I could give it back just as fast, just as furious.

But love? Love was brutal. Considering how strongly I felt it, I didn't say it much. Love, my peeps, hurt, *especially* when those you felt it for left you when you least expected it.

"Will you do something for me?" he asked, interrupting my thoughts.

His words and deep tone drew me back to reality and for the moment, dissolved my fears. I climbed on top of him and pressed my lips against his for a brief kiss. "I'll do anything for you."

Gem moaned when I swiveled my hips yet surprised me when he rolled me back onto my side. His face flushed slightly, and he gave me a half-embarrassed laugh. "That's not what I mean," he said, digging his fingers through my hair and stroking my scalp.

"Then wassup?" I pushed out my bottom lip. "You left me for ten days. I figured we needed to make up for our time apart."

He tugged on that lip with his teeth, an indication that round three would soon start. Instead he pulled back, watching me with tremendous interest. "I want you to meet my parents."

If I had a penis, it would have immediately gone limp then.

2

____

I briefly entertained the thought of hurtling myself out the window and running away screaming. Was he kidding? I wasn't the kind of gal men brought home to mom. I was the kind they had sex with. Lots of sex. And, not to brag, I was good at it. My hold slowly slipped away. "What?" I managed.

The corners of his mouth lifted. "I said I want you to meet my parents. They've just returned from Japan, where they met with Elders of the remaining packs and—"

"You want me to meet your parents?"

He didn't miss a beat, ignoring the shrill tone of my voice. "Yes."

I scrambled out of bed. "No. I'm sorry. Anything but that." My heart was pounding through my chest. _Holy shit. He wants me to meet his parents. Holy shit, what's happening here? Holy shit, weren't we just having fun?_

"Holy shit," I said out loud.

"Taran, what's wrong?"

"Baby, I don't know about this." I reached for my discarded panties on the floor before I remembered he'd torn them off with his teeth.

"Taran, tell me why you're so upset."

Most girls would just spill their guts and answer, but most girls hadn't had it rough—not like me. They hadn't watched their parents die in front of them or been shoved into foster care where they were groped, mistreated, and harmed. I had walls up for a reason. I needed to protect myself against pain. I always told myself a serious relationship could only lead to just that. And knowing this, what did I go ahead and do? Fall in love.

I covered my face with my hands, wondering when Gemini and I became what we were. At first, I only intended to have a fling. Next thing I knew he moved in. We didn't really talk about it. It just happened. I didn't fight it because I wanted him with me. But this . . . Where were we going here?

Someplace I was too afraid to venture, that's for sure.

"I can't believe you're serious about this," I managed.

"You can't believe I'm serious about my family and my desire for you to meet them, or how much I love you?" He leaned back on his hands when my teeth clenched tight. "I realize you don't want to discuss this—"

"So then let's not, please."

He shook his head. "No, let's. It's only fair that you tell me what this is really about."

"It's not about anything. Just something I don't do, like, ever." I waggled my finger at him. "And you know I've done some kinky shit."

He didn't appreciate my attempt at humor. If anything, he seemed more upset. *Damn it.*

"You've never met anyone's parents because you've never had a relationship that lasted more than a handful of days. We've been together several months. I know you don't like to talk about how serious we've become, or accept what you mean to me, but I think it's time that you start."

"I thought you liked me as I am," I offered, grasping at straws. "Weren't you the same wolf who called me perfect?"

"You are perfect to me, and for me." He straightened. "I'm not asking you to change or to assume a different role. But I do want to close the distance that remains between us."

Gemini was aware of my past from the tidbits here and there I managed to share. But they weren't long, drawn-out conversations. I didn't break down and cry. I didn't bleed my soul to him. Could I have? Yeah. In truth, I could have cried for days and spilled enough details to make him tear this room apart. But I didn't, knowing that what happened to me would infuriate and upset him, mostly because he wasn't around to protect me. So instead, I spoke of these incidences like they didn't matter, and like they were long forgotten.

Even though they weren't.

The trauma of my past kept us from growing closer, but in a way, I was grateful for that space. That space kept me safe.

Or so I reasoned.

Instead of admitting as much, I closed up emotionally and opened myself up physically. Physical was easier than revealing what lies beneath the surface, especially for me.

I sashayed forward and ran my nails down his muscular chest. "You want to close some distance between us?" I asked, my voice dripping with desire. "Then what say we get back in bed and get back to business."

Gem grabbed my wrists before I could move them further south. He kissed the backs of my hands and stared at me intently. "Taran, you are my mate . . ."

The whole "mate" thing always made me uncomfortable and struck my protective walls like a sledgehammer. I tried to pull away, but he held tight.

". . . and therefore, the most important being in the world to me," he continued patiently. "Do me the honor of letting me introduce you to my parents."

"Babe, this isn't a good idea," I said, holding my ground. I stepped away and out of his reach. My past held me back, that was true. But I couldn't tell him as much. What I could do was point out what he failed to see of my present. "Look at me. When I walk into a club, or even a restaurant, you know what most people think?"

"That you're beautiful," he answered. There was no hesitation in his voice, but he'd always been good to me. Society as a whole had not.

"No. They think 'stripper.'" I pointed to the girls. "They take one look at these and my ass and that's all they see. Do you have any idea how many times men *and* women have asked me if I do porn? Do you think they care if I'm a nurse? Or that I can save lives? Or that I actually have a heart? I've had couples offer to pay me for sex."

Gemini squared his jaw. He'd seen men leer at me and attempt to approach me if they saw him leave my side. It was one of the reasons I didn't venture out much without him. Don't get me wrong, before hooking up with Gemini, I used to enjoy all the attention—the good kind, I mean—those nights of dancing with sexy men, and steamy bedroom romps. The assholes I didn't miss one bit. But since meeting my wolf, the fulfillment and attention my appearance once brought me didn't matter anymore. Only Gem did. When I'd go out, it was usually with him. Humans, although unaware the supernatural world existed, sensed the predator within him and kept a safe distance in his presence.

"Why are you being so hard on yourself?" he asked, bringing me back to the moment. "You're stunning. It's not something to be ashamed of, neither is the desire you evoke."

That wasn't what he thought the time a werecheetah grabbed my ass. Boyfriend had slammed the spotted idiot to the floor by the throat and crushed his larynx. "I'm not ashamed of the way I look. But you're not asking me to meet your buddies, or a co-worker, or an old friend from college, are you?"

"I'm not. But what difference does it make who they are?"

I slapped my hands against my sides. "You're kidding, right? Gemini, I'm not the kind of woman men bring home to Mom. I'm the kind that moms fear their sons will bring home."

"You're wrong."

My throat tightened. "No. You are," I told him truthfully. "A pal, someone you work with—I actually stand a shot at impressing him or her. But even if I don't"— I groaned—"I wouldn't care. You're asking me to meet your parents. Your *parents*."

He leaned forward to rest his forearms against his knees and released a deep sigh. "I realize this, Taran. But what you fail to see is my reason for introducing you to them. Someday, when you're ready, you will be my bride—"

"Don't," I said cutting him off. "You know it's not something I can talk about."

The instant I said it, I regretted it. I'll be the first to admit that I can be extremely bitchy. But I'm not a bitch. I hated hurting him.

Yet I had to be honest. Marriage wasn't something I never considered, even with him. Marriage was a final blow to my defenses that I couldn't allow. Not if I was going to spare what remained of my heart.

He rose and looked at me for a beat before storming into the bathroom. For as quiet as he could be, I heard every harsh slap of his bare feet across the dark wood floor.

I buried my face in my hands. *Shit. What did I do?*

I waited a few minutes after I heard the shower start running before following him, not bothering to dress. My actions were deliberate. Short of the cursed gold that sickened and killed most preternaturals, decapitation, and the destruction of his heart, Gemini didn't have many weaknesses. Yet my naked body topped that short list. And didn't I need it then?

Was it immature, manipulative, unfair? Maybe. But like I said, surrendering physically was way easier for me. So, I used my strengths, and yeah, yeah, my big girls, too.

Light steam greeted me as I slipped into the bathroom. I strode toward him, watching him through the clear glass doors. He passed his soapy hands along his muscular torso and then down each arm. I leaned against the wall, the cobalt-blue tile feeling cool against my skin as I waited for him to turn my way. He knew I was there. He always sensed me near. But he seemed to need a moment, so that's exactly what I gave him.

White foam cascaded down his form in quick waves. I watched, admired, and waited. But it was only when he rinsed off his face that he finally glanced my way. Rather than giving me his usual slow appraising look, he averted his stare, pressing his hands against the wall of glass and leaning forward to allow the water to pound against his back.

Okay, wasn't expecting *that* response. Wow. My nipples were stiff and everything.

Fine. Plan B it is. I strolled forward and knocked softly against the glass. "Mind if I join you?"

Streams of water trickled down his face, but his attention fixed on the frosted glass window a few feet away and well away from me. "I'm almost done. I'll be out in a minute if you want to step in."

I stood there positively dumbstruck and *hurt*. Didn't he know I wanted to feel close to him, even if it wasn't in the way he'd intended?

His rebuff physically pained me. I crossed my arms and bowed my head. "Baby, please don't be mad. Meeting your parents is just something I'm not comfortable doing."

He shut off the water and stepped out, reaching for a white towel. "I'm not angry, Taran. I'm disappointed."

My heart sank. "Oh, okay. That's not worse or anything."

He passed the towel along his skin in quick motions. "What do you expect, Taran? You tell me you love me, yet you refuse to allow me to claim you as my mate, and now—"

"Oh, you mean like when Aric claimed Celia?" My hurt was kicked to the curb, and in its place a very pissed-off Jersey girl remained. "That's something that's supposed to be sacred to your kind."

"It is," he growled.

I jutted out my chin. "If that's true, why did your alpha dump my sister after he claimed her?" I threw out my hands. "If this claim binds them—if it's so hallowed—how could he walk away so easily?"

I have a temper. A bad one. And that temper rises faster than the strike of a match when it comes to those I most love. Celia, like me, had walls as thick as granite shielding her heart. She made the mistake of opening them up to Aric, and it cost her. Big time. He more than broke that heart; he crushed her soul when he left her.

Gemini straightened to his full six-foot-plus frame. "It wasn't easy for him to leave her, Taran. It remains his biggest burden and regret."

I lifted my chin. "And yet he still did it. You call me your mate. You want to claim me. But Celia and Aric are living proof that it does nothing. What's the point of being linked for eternity if you won't even stay with the person you're bonded to?"

The anger creasing Gemini's frown lessened in severity. "Just because they're no longer together doesn't make their love less real, nor their bond less strong. Celia will always be Aric's mate. He'll never love another."

I nodded. "Really? I'm sure that evil fiancée of his would love to hear that."

He swiped his hand across his face. "Taran, we've discussed this. Aric is a pureblood werewolf. He is held in a different regard than I am. He is obligated to continue our race, and that means reproducing with another pureblood."

"I'm sure knowing that is a tremendous comfort to Celia."

He dropped the towel and gathered me to him. He was naked. And Gemini naked usually led to crazy sex. But for once, that was the last thing I wanted. "You may not believe me, but your sister is important to me, and a friend. I feel for her pain." He stroked my cheek softly. "I can't imagine being forced to stay away from the one I love."

I leaned in close. Although my anger and reservations lingered, I didn't want to fight with him. My wolf meant everything to me. We needed to talk, even though I didn't care for the conversation. "Why is claiming me so important to you, anyway?"

He cocked his head, as if unsure he understood my question. "It's the way my wolves and I officially proclaim our mate. Our promise to love only one partner for eternity."

"Isn't it enough to just say it?" I meant that. Why did it have to be such a big leap? I was committed. He knew I saw and wanted only him.

He surprised me by smiling softly. "Perhaps if I were human what we have would be enough. But I'm not. It's important to me as a *were*. Much like marriage is to some, but instead of exchanging rings, our souls become one."

Oh. Soul bonding. Awesome. That couldn't possibly end in disaster or anything.

I covered my face with my hands, convinced I wouldn't survive this whole commitment thing without ending up on the floor, writhing in agony. Emme and Celia would be jumping for joy to hear such words from their loves—exactly like Shayna had when she skipped down the aisle with Koda. But I wasn't "that" kind of girl. You know those girls who came out of the womb picking out their china, who always dreamed of their wedding days—where it would be, what their dress would look like, who would attend to them?

Yeah. I always made fun of them.

A girl I knew in high school flat-out told me she wanted to be married by twenty-four and have her first child—a boy, I think she said—by the time she was twenty-six.

Girlfriend didn't mention she'd be divorced by the time she was twenty-seven. I saw a picture of her on Facebook recently. She was a shell of her former self following her devastating breakup. Like Celia, was that what would eventually become of me?

Regardless of what Gemini said about not being obliged by his pack to breed with another *were,* with the war being what it was, that could all change. And where would that leave me? Like Aric, Gemini would have to obey his Elders, no matter who it crushed.

I ran my fingers through my hair. All this mating and marriage talk scared me. Like literally left me shaking, because I saw what happened when it didn't work out. Lord Almighty, hadn't I hurt enough?

And yet as much as it frightened me and made me want to pull away, I wasn't blind to what it meant to him. "How would you do it, exactly? How would you claim me?"

Gemini's eyes smoldered, causing my head to snap back. *Whoa, baby.* He lifted my chin and kissed me with so much heat, the points of my breasts saluted him. I just about jumped up and straddled him again. But that wasn't what he wanted.

"During our lovemaking, I'll ask to have you, and give myself to you in return," he said. "Before we finish, I'll proclaim you as mine."

It didn't sound too complicated. In fact, it sounded kind of hot. Still, my defenses rushed to the surface to protect me, like I'd conditioned them to. "What if it doesn't work?" *And all this wasn't real,* I don't add.

"The only time a claim fails is when a *were* tries it on someone who's not truly his or her mate," he patiently explained. "A claim won't work if there's someone else I'm meant to love more."

"So, it's possible, right?" My voice trails. "That I may not be the one?"

Gemini pulled away, chuckling, and reached for his shorts. He slipped them on and shook out his slacks, all the while smiling at me. Well, at least someone was sure of himself. "My wolves recognized you as ours from the first moment we saw you," he said like it was obvious. "Or have you forgotten our initial attraction?"

How could I forget that? The first night I met Gem, I was completely entranced by him. I thought initially that he was pulling some kind of wolf mojo on me. I could barely speak, and I couldn't stop myself from staring at those ever watchful eyes. Sparks from my own magic literally flew and at one point, I felt like I was having some sort of mystical climax.

"No." I lowered my head and flicked my long nails. "I remember."

He finished dressing as he watched me. This time, he knew I was the one requiring a serious moment. I thought I should shower, dress, or something to maybe stretch out the time I needed. But the minute I glanced up, his strong arms embraced me. "You're afraid you're not my mate, aren't you?"

I was afraid of a lot of things then—that I wasn't his mate, but even more so that I might be. If matehood was true, and its "claim" bonded *souls,* that was a whole different level of commitment and pain I was setting myself up for.

"I never figured myself to be the committed type," I confessed. "This just makes everything so official, so . . ."

Gem raised his dark eyebrows. "Real?" he offered.

"Dangerous," I countered.

That went over like most kicks to the balls. Hurt shadowed his face, and maybe mine, too.

Life, like I mentioned, had dealt me and my sisters a cruel hand. In a way, we'd grown accustomed to the bad, and the not so great. But the cruelty we'd faced had screwed us up in countless ways, making us bleed tears that burned their way down to our hearts.

I closed my eyes, trying to shake that familiar sense of impending doom. I didn't want to hurt anymore. But I might. What I felt for Gemini packed enough punch to drive me to my knees. Tack on the claim he desired to weld us with, and he would destroy me if he walked away.

Maybe that was why I was so against meeting Mom and Pop Hamamatsu—they represented another step onto the Heartbreak Express.

I lifted my lids, my blue eyes traveling to meet Gem's dark ones. "I'm not ready to be mated. I'm not ready to meet your parents. It's not that I want to be with anyone else. I'm just not comfortable with what it means, or represents, or what it could lead to."

He clasped my elbows, stroking them lightly. "I don't understand your fear. The claim won't alter you or us. It will only strengthen what's already there."

What Gemini considered strengthening, I viewed as weakening a part of me I couldn't leave vulnerable. When I spoke, I could barely get the words out. "This connection . . . this claim, it's the equivalent of marriage to your kind, isn't it?"

He paused as if debating whether or not to answer. In the end, he told me the truth, refusing to lie, although I'd probably have preferred lies to honesty then. "Yes. All who are *were* would consider us married."

So not what I needed to hear. "Is this why you want me to meet your parents? You're hoping it will change my mind or something?"

"Taran, I'm not trying to force you into a corner. But while you try to play off what's between us as nothing more than a casual relationship—one we both could walk away from—it's not. You are my mate. I want to present you as such and solidify what you mean to me."

My heart was beating way too fast considering we were only talking. "By claiming me, right? I mean, that's what it's all coming down to."

"Our claim is something I deeply desire as a *were* and as a man." The knuckles of his hand skimmed along my arm. "And that desire grows each time I'm with you."

I forced my next words out. "If I do this—if I agree to allow this bond—will *you* consider us married?"

"I will. But we can postpone the actual ceremony—"

I stepped away from him, my eyes welling. "I can't do this."

He dropped his hands to his sides. "Which part?"

"All of it. Baby, we've only known each other a handful of months."

He averted his gaze, shaking his head. "Taran, don't use our brief time together as an excuse. I know what I feel. And even if I gave you years, I doubt your excuses would be any different."

Who says we'd make it years? For all I knew, his Elders would order him to leave me as early as tomorrow, or he'd walk away without another glance back. But I don't tell him this because for me, I've already said too much. "I can't," was all could offer.

The expression of sadness frozen on his features made my tears run faster. "All right," he said. "You're clearly not ready for what I'm offering, so for now, let's drop it."

My voice splintered like glass. "You're pissed at me, aren't you?"

In not answering right away he said enough, despite his next few words. "I don't want to pressure you, and I don't want to fight. But I won't pretend that your response doesn't affect me."

He gave me his back and finished dressing. Tears drenched my cheeks as I watched him. He was the perfect blend of man and hero, and it didn't matter. I couldn't give him what he wanted.

He straightened slowly from pulling on his socks, his back still to me. He couldn't stand to see me cry. Yet I knew that he was hurting, too.

"I'm sorry," I whispered when he faced me.

"I'm sorry, too," he said, once more gathering me to him and curling his long body over mine. "I don't want to dwell on this. And I'll never force you to do something against your will. But I want to feel closer to you. Please, at least consider meeting my parents. It would mean a great deal to me, and to them as well."

He waited until I settled, then started for the door.

"Where are you going?" I asked, worried he could no longer stand to be around me. "I thought you didn't have to work today."

He withdrew the phone from his pocket. "Aric sent a text. A local pack on the Nevada side found evidence that suggests demons. He requests my presence for a meeting with the local clan of witches to see what course of action we should take, and to see if we need to involve the vampires at this time."

I didn't want to but asked anyway. "What kind of evidence?"

His features darkened. "The fresh remains of two humans."

3

Gemini left our room following a brief kiss goodbye, leaving me with thoughts of demon children flapping their naked wings and the horrendous turn our day had taken.

Just a month prior, we'd succeeded in rescuing my sisters from a Tribe stronghold and a fate worse than death. Death by demon impregnation and delivery of said creature was the last way *anyone* deserved to go.

I shuddered and jumped into the shower to wash the disturbing memories of those demon children raking their claws against me, their long forked tongues flicking against my cheek, greedy for a taste of my insides. My skin crawled as I passed the loofah sponge along my body. I scrubbed hard, their nasty images flooding my mind and refusing to leave me.

My nightmares had warned me they were coming. That didn't prepare me, though, for everything that happened. I was practically paralyzed with fear during the attack, and although I'd resented the backfire curse that had triggered our powers, it helped saved me, and ultimately my sisters.

I stepped out of the shower, drying my body quickly and

reaching for the lotion. The shower relaxed me and succeeded in erasing my disgusting and twisted memories. What it didn't do was help me shake the disappointment shadowing Gemini's features.

I wasn't perfect. I knew that. But I never pretended to be perfect. Did I swear? Hell yeah. Was I inappropriate? Most sailors thought so. Did I have an attitude? Possibly. But if nothing else, I stayed true to who I was. My dilemma remained that who I was, was someone Gemini's ultratraditional Japanese parents wouldn't like. That I was sure of.

Couldn't my wolf see that I'd only jeopardize his relationship with them?

And couldn't he see how scared I was to meet them?

As I finished drying my hair, I realized I could have handled things differently, although I wasn't sure exactly how given my insecurities and fears. So, I did what I did best: made myself look good on the outside so I'd feel better about how I felt on the inside.

I pulled on a skintight sweater dress and thigh-high boots and strutted out of my room and into the kitchen, where Emme's boyfriend, Liam, yapped away. Emme sat on a barstool, her small frame appearing to wilt as she suffered through another one of Liam's hunting tales. I shook my head and tried not to grimace. That boy was going to make her a vegetarian if he told one more disembowelment story.

Liam didn't seem to notice the green tone to her pallor as he enthusiastically continued his spellbinding tale. ". . . and then I tore into his hide like it was made of paper. Warm blood pooled in my jaws, spilling down my fur—ever have warm blood squirt in your mouth?" He didn't wait for Emme to answer. "Greatest feeling ever—oh, and you should have seen how big his stomach was when I ripped it open with my fangs." He laughed. "Somebody liked salmon, let me tell you—"

Emme whipped her head toward me. While she possessed

the power to heal, her ability evidently couldn't soothe her mounting nausea. She clutched her belly, swallowing hard. "Hi, Taran."

That was what she said. What she really meant was, "Make him stop." I tried not to laugh, but she really needed to tell him how much she hated these graphic accounts, rather than trying to be so supportive. I drew closer and spread her soft blond hair around her shoulders. "Hey, sweetie," I told her.

Her smile returned some of the color to her fair skin. "You look nice," she said quietly. "Are you going out?"

I released her hair, focusing on the splash of freckles along the bridge of her nose. Emme was almost twenty-three, but her gentle disposition made her seem and look younger. I never had her innocence, like, ever. If she wasn't my sister, I doubt she'd hang out with the likes of me. But she was, and she did. And I knew I was blessed because of it.

"Yeah. I have stuff to do," I answered, inching away from her.

In all actuality, I meant to talk with her and Shayna, and get some insight on what to do about Gemini. But Liam had this thing: Hunting made him horny. He bounced off the walls whenever he returned from a mission, and then quickly bounced along with Emme between the sheets. His beast, so riled from chasing prey, usually alternated between bringing home bucks and banging Emme. It didn't take a genius to see my youngest sister preferred the latter. And seeing how Shayna and Koda were newly married, they were all about the banging, too.

Shayna fiddled at the center island, using her ability to manipulate metal to sharpen a knife and cut into a chunk of meat the size of a toddler. She dropped the piece into a broiler pan, her long black ponytail swinging as she quickly seasoned it. But when she tried to heft the sucker in her arms, she almost dropped it.

Koda easily lifted the pan from her grasp and crossed the kitchen to place it into the oven. "Thanks, puppy," she told him, lighting up the room with her grin. She skipped, I kid you not, right into his arms. I may have been all attitude, but Shayna was all perk and pep, "woo-hooing" her way right into the big brute's heart.

Speaking of hearts . . . there was one the size of my skull on a serving plate. *What the?* My eyes skimmed along our granite countertops. Butchered meat topped every casserole dish and pot we owned. A leg here, an organ there. It was like a twisted episode of *CSI*.

Shayna turned to me and forced a smile. "We're having *bear* for dinner tonight," she explained.

My lips slowly parted as I turned back to Liam. "You're welcome," he said with a grin.

What do you say to that? Seriously? I edged away from a bowl overflowing with insides.

"Something wrong, T?" Shayna asked me.

"Besides the carnage?" I asked. I tried not to gag, but the row of intestines shining beside me on a silver platter shot that attempt to hell. I shuddered. "I was going to ask you about something"—crap; that liver poking through our Crock-Pot was the size of my thigh—"but I don't want to interfere with all this foodie stuff you have going on so I'll take a ride over to see Celia."

"You're going to see the leeches," Koda said.

He wasn't happy. Wow, now there was a big ol' shock coming from the guy who probably flossed his fangs with wire. I crossed my arms. "I'm going to see my sister. You remember Celia? She used to live here before your pussy werewolf alpha dumped her."

Koda's tumultuous dark eyes squared on mine. "Don't call him that."

"You mean a pussy?" I liked Koda. Truly I did. He treated

Shayna like a precious stone. That said, he couldn't be mad at the vamps or at Celia for shacking up with them. Aric didn't leave her with much of a choice after he left, did he?

"T, knock it off," Shayna said. She left his arms and led me out of the kitchen, far from her walking building of a husband. She didn't want us to fight. But Koda didn't scare me.

Much.

Okay. In all fairness he scared everyone but Shayna.

Emme slipped from the barstool and quickly followed.

"What's wrong, dude?" Shayna asked, her blue irises appearing to see right through me. "You seem off."

I was, but I couldn't tell them about Gemini just then. So, I switched gears. "Did you hear about those humans who were found dead?"

Shayna nodded, causing her long black ponytail to bop behind her. "Yup. Koda says they're fresh kills. He and Liam are going to lead a team after dinner if the pack currently scouting doesn't find something first." She considered me. Her pixie face riddled with concern. "Is that all?"

I shrugged. "Isn't that enough?"

"Well, yes, but . . ." She considered me. "What's bugging you, T? For reals?"

I must have looked worse than I thought. "Nothing that can't wait." I pretended to glance at the hall clock. "I have to run. I'll talk to you two later."

I shrugged into my coat and grabbed my keys from the small table, then walked outside and onto our front porch. Shayna and Emme followed, catching up to me at the bottom of the steps. Emme clasped my hand. "Is this about Gemini?" She nibbled on her bottom lip. "I don't mean to pry, but he seemed upset when he left."

My attention shifted in the direction of Lake Tahoe when the breeze carried traces of its magic to brush against my cheek.

I meant to insist nothing was up, but I waited too long to answer.

"Liam and I aren't doing that great, either," she admitted.

"What?" both Shayna and I said.

Shayna reached for her hand. "But-but, he's like totally into you. And aside from the"— forcing a swallow— "bagging-the-bear thingy, he's barely left your side."

Emme focused hard on her feet, even though there was nothing there. "Don't get me wrong. He's good to me, and he loves me—I know he does." She lifted her gaze, her attention alternating between me and Shayna. "But it's not the same way your wolves love you. I can see it. And I'm starting to feel it."

"Then he doesn't know what he has," I told her. I gathered Emme in a warm hug, hating how sad she seemed. Liam adored her. That much was obvious. But I understood what she meant. As much as he showered her with affection, it was different from the way Koda practically worshipped Shayna . . . and yeah, how maybe Gemini treated me, too.

Jesus. What was I going to do about my wolf?

I released her then, unsure what to say to offer her comfort.

Fortunately, Shayna's peppy inner cheerleader always had something positive to shake her pom-poms at. "Em, Liam's already talking about Christmas and Valentine's Day and next summer. Doesn't that say he's thinking about forever with you?"

"It's not that his love is dwindling, or that he isn't committed." Emme shook her head. "It's more like his love can't go any further than what it is, if that makes sense."

Shayna crinkled her brow, unable to understand. But she was very much spinning in postmarital bliss. It was all frolicking kittens and humping ponies as far as she was concerned. "I know he loves you," she insisted.

True. But sometimes it wasn't enough.

Something in my features must have given me away. Both exchanged glances before returning their full attention on me.

"T, what is it?" Shayna asked. "You look seconds from losing it."

I forced down my worry and plastered a phony grin on my face. "Nothing that can't wait," I answered. "Right now, you need to get back to your woolly mammoth and you, Miss Emme, need to go back to story time."

Shayna laughed at Emme's grimace. I guessed Emme was hoping I'd save her from more of Liam's riveting tales of disembowelment and decapitation.

I kept my grin in place, reaching to play with her hair again. "He loves you, baby girl. He really does," I said.

"Thanks, Taran." A glimmer of hope lit up her eyes. I always told it to her straight, so maybe the words meant more coming from me. But when her hands squeezed mine, I knew I wasn't completely off the hook. "Are you sure nothing's wrong? You seem so disheartened."

I lifted my chin, working to hang on to my smile. "Positive. I just need some Celia time. It's not the same around here without her."

"No, it's not," both Emme and Shayna agreed.

Emme pushed a strand of her blond hair behind her ear. "Will you be back for dinner? Maybe we can talk more then."

I thought about the remains of the autopsy scattered along the kitchen. "Sure. Wouldn't miss it," I bit out.

Before they could say anything more, I strutted down our walk and into the driveway, thinking I could make a quick and uneventful exit.

"*Taran Wird!* Must you dress like the devil's slut?"

I thought wrong.

Mrs. Mancuso was hands-down the worst neighbor in history, and the biggest pain in the ass in support hose. The cold breeze sweeping in from the lake flapped her neck skin like a sail, but the chill it brought had nothing on her stare. My nips could have snapped clear off from the coldness darkening her beady eyes. I took a few deliberate steps in her direction, only to have Emme clasp my arm and pull me back. "Taran," my sister pleaded. "For once, just count to ten and ignore her."

I considered Emme's plea. For about two-point-five seconds, until Mancuso trained her glare on Shayna when Shayna offered a friendly grin and a wave. "What's your problem?" I asked the old hag. Seriously, Shayna was just being nice. "Did you wake up on the wrong side of the crypt this morning?"

Her beady eyes narrowed. "No. I just live next to harlots," she answered.

Here's the thing: Say what you want about me, but don't mess with those I love. "Zip it, you old coot!" I shot back. "Don't you have Snow White to poison?"

Emme groaned as Mancuso abandoned the broom, she was using to sweep her walkway and edged to her property line. "Give me one reason I shouldn't kick your skinny ass," she challenged.

I threw out a hand. "Um, I don't know. Maybe cause you'd trip over your neck skin, break a hip, and lose your dentures?"

Shayna leapt in front of me. "She's just kidding, Mrs. M." Shayna always tried to keep the peace, but her comment only earned her a stiff middle finger in addition to the one Mrs. Mancuso was already waving at me. If she could have managed, she probably would have flipped Emme off with her toes. There was evil, and then there was Mrs. Mancuso. Most demons wouldn't have stood a chance against this walking ad for adult diapers.

I watched her walk away, probably in search of puppies to kick, her middle fingers still high in the air. What had I ever done to deserve Mancuso?

Emme shook her head. "You weren't very nice to her."

To which I frowned and answered, "She started it." Hey, I was all kinds of mature.

Emme sighed. "Now, Taran, you know if anything ever happened to her, you would feel terrible."

I thought about it. "Nope. Not even a little bit." I kissed her cheek, then Shayna's, before slipping into my sedan and starting the engine with a roar.

Shayna tapped on the glass. "Be careful, T. Koda says there's suspected demon activity in the area. We might have made a huge dent in the population, but those Tribe members who survived are still out there. Stay sharp and stay close." Her bright eyes dulled. "I don't want them to get you, too . . ."

4

My Subaru Legacy drove up the mile-long road that led to Misha's compound, rolling to a stop in front of the tall metal gates that opened onto his estate. Stone walls lined the exterior, with gargoyle heads sprouting every few feet. High-tech cameras were placed within the creepy critters' gaping maws. After losing so many vamps in his keep, Misha wanted to see all, know all. He also wanted to harness the perfect weapon.

And that weapon was Celia.

A vamp materialized from nowhere. Okay, that wasn't entirely true. Vampires couldn't vanish and reappear; more like they were outrageously sneaky. But his movements were so quick, so silent, it was like he was just suddenly there.

He smiled at me through my passenger-side window. I smiled back but kept my guard up. "Good afternoon, miss," he whispered with as much sex in his tone as found in most pornos. "Are you here to see Master Aleksandr?"

"No. I'm here to see Celia Wird."

"In that case . . ." I didn't see him reach in and flick the locks, his movements too fast to register. He flung open the door, reaching for me.

The air sizzled as bolts of blue and white lightning shot from my fingertips and into the vamp, sending him soaring. I stepped out of the car and cracked my knuckles, feeding off the energetic boost my power gave me.

Fang boy flapped, crackled, and smoked against the asphalt. I held back only because he belonged to Misha. Had he been an unknown vamp, the only thing left would have been a pile of ash.

I didn't appreciate him trying to take a bite or attempting to use his hypnotic crap on me. Had I been human, I would have been easy prey, a thought that only riled my anger.

The vamp's stupor was short-lived. He leapt to his feet, bounding forward. *Okay, fricasseed vamp it is.* My vision sharpened and my hands trembled with energy. I lifted them, aimed, and—

Another vamp catapulted over the gate, sweeping the vamp charging me up by the throat, his sharp nails puncturing through the skin. Tim, one of Misha's bodyguards, had arrived.

Tim held the vamp about two feet off the ground. "You fool," he hissed. "This is Celia's sister." Blood seeped from the corners of the vamp's mouth as he spoke. "She's under the master's protection and not to be touched."

Thing was, despite how vulnerable Gemini had left me, I didn't want to be protected or coddled then. "Put him down, Tim." I flashed him a wicked smile. "I'm having a bad day. Wouldn't mind relieving some of that stress, you feel me?"

Tim dropped him like a stone and kicked him about thirty feet away, stepping in front of me when I stomped forward. "Let it go, Taran. He's new. It won't happen again."

"Spoilsport," I said with a sarcastic pout.

That earned me a sexy grin. "Sorry to ruin your fun," Tim

said, circling. He eyed me from my fluffy hair to my high-heeled boots. "Nice. Real nice. You still seeing that mutt?"

I leaned in and tapped his chin with my fingertip. "Be nice when you talk about my wolf, Tim, or I'll tell Misha you insulted me."

Tim's face paled even though I was kidding. When it came down to it, all the vamps in Misha's keep adored him. He was their master and the world seemed to halt at the very sight of his god-like presence. All worshipping aside, they were scared senseless of him. I couldn't blame them. Even long before Celia inadvertently returned his soul, Misha's power stroked my skin like a warm and dangerous caress.

Tim cleared his throat. "Maybe we should head inside. I'm sure your lovely sister can't wait to see you."

Lovely sister? I rolled my eyes, knowing what he and the other vamps really thought of Celia. "Yes. I think that would be best."

I slid back into my car but paused when a flapping sound stirred my senses. I jerked my head to the left, where a thick patch of trees stretched along the opposite side of the road. "Did you hear that?" I asked Tim.

Tim clenched his fists. "Yeah. I did."

One vamp, two vamps, three vamps, four. They leapt over the stone wall like a bunch of frogs with fangs. He lifted his chin and as simply as that, they were off. "They'll check the premises. Let's get you inside the compound."

"I can help." My voice was oddly vacant. For all I meant that I'd follow the vamps through those dark trees, it didn't mean I wasn't scared.

Tim shook his head, but his attention remained further ahead. "The master remains your protector. Nothing is supposed to happen to you, especially on his land. Get inside. They'll report back."

He shut the car door at the same time the gates began to

part. I drove through, a familiar unease raking down my spine like the point of a dagger. Tim took off in a slow jog that turned into a blur of speed. Despite the designer dress shoes he wore, he barely made a sound as his feet struck against the blue slate double-wide driveway.

The moment I cut the engine and unlocked the door, Tim was opening it for me. He motioned toward the main doors. "I'll give you an update as soon as I have one. In the meantime, Celia's in the kitchen eating lunch with the master."

Although I was unnerved by what waited just outside vamp camp, I stopped and gawked at him. "Damn, Tim. Are you serious? He's sucking someone dry while she's nibbling on a sandwich?"

Tim laughed despite the tension stiffening his shoulders. "No, hot stuff. He doesn't feed in front of her. Besides, you know we only take about a pint."

I shuddered. I was a nurse by trade and could handle blood, but that didn't mean I wanted to drink it. I hopped up the steps to the main doors. Two more vamps appeared and opened them for me, permitting me access into a massive foyer with a cathedral-style timbered ceiling. They gave me the once-over, flashing a little fang with their grins. I groaned. Although it had been a few weeks, I still couldn't get used to the fact that my sister was shacked up with a master vampire.

The heels of my tall boots stomped against the blocks of bluestone that made up the floor. A few vamps loitered with their meals, laughing with and teasing their enamored humans. A particularly leggy blonde watched her vamp with lustful eyes, hungry for that orgasmic rush the feed would bring her. I didn't see the point—at least not from her perspective. She would be influenced to forget the experience, and the supernatural world along with it.

Personally, I preferred to remember my toe-curling orgasms.

The vamp lengthened his fangs, stroking the blonde's jugular while his stare lifted to meet mine as I neared. "Hey, Taran," Hank said. "You look—"

I batted my hand. "Yeah, yeah, good enough to eat. Save it for someone you can actually snack on."

I flounced past him and down the hall that led into the enormous French-inspired kitchen, stopping in the arched entryway. Just as Tim had said, there was Celia. I removed my coat and tugged on the hem of my sweater dress. The scoop neck fell just above the swells of my breasts.

My ensemble was sexy, and like most of my clothes, fashionable. But it didn't matter. At least, not to Misha.

Celia sat crossed-legged on a chair like a little kid, wearing her usual tank top and shin-length yoga pants. No makeup. No cute clothes. And long, wavy hair wrangled into a messy ponytail.

Yet she held the hottest guy with fangs completely captivated. I smiled to myself. Celia was beautiful without even trying. Maybe it was her palpable strength or her kind heart. Or maybe it was simply the way her smile reached her green eyes despite the sadness that hovered beneath the surface.

I shook my head. Her problem was that she never considered herself desirable. It wasn't her fault. Her inner tigress scared anything human and made her unapproachable. That changed when a certain sexy vampire and a royal-among-werewolves crossed her path.

Too bad that royal werewolf turned into a royal douche.

Celia straightened and her face lit up when I stepped out from beneath the archway.

"Hey. What are you doing here?" she asked.

I shrugged. "Just wanted to surprise you." Truthfully, I didn't call or text because I wanted to catch her unprepared—see if she was really "all right" as she claimed. My sisters and I, hey, and our friends, too, were worried about

Celia. Not just because of the whole Aric fiasco, but because of who she turned to during her lowest point.

Misha caught the underlying white lie beneath my half-truth. He raised an elegant brow but didn't call me on it. "Good afternoon, Taran," he said, the allure in his voice sweeping along my skin to cop a feel. He took in my appearance, giving a rather long and thorough glance.

You're not so enamored with Celia, are you, Drac?

No sooner did the thought cross my mind than his eyes wandered back to her. I couldn't help my laugh, knowing that short of standing there naked I was no match for Little Miss Golden Tigress.

Misha rose, cutting Celia off when she was almost to me. Tim was suddenly there. Man, that super speed really wigged me out. "Nothing, Master," he said.

"You're certain?" Misha asked him.

"A full sweep was conducted. No presence of demons was detected."

"Demons?" Celia asked, her attention cutting to me.

I shrugged like it was no biggie, even though I struggled to keep from cringing. "We heard some flapping outside the gates. And, ah, a couple of eaten humans were discovered on the Nevada side. The *weres* suspect demons and such."

Yeah. That went over well.

"It was probably a bird—an owl or something," I offered when her tigress eyes replaced her human ones. It was a trick she'd pulled more than once, but it gave me pause every time.

Celia lulled her tigress back to sleep, her normal eyes returning once more to meet Tim's gaze. "The vamps didn't see or smell *anything* unusual?"

He waited before responding. "No. If anything was there, it's gone now."

"Set up patrols outside the grounds," Misha said in a tone that sounded easy, but was packed to the gills with command.

"Yes, Master," Tim responded.

His disappearance seemed to lift the tension the word *demon* had stirred. For all their power, demons and their babies avoided Tahoe's magic like poison. And Misha's pad had a front-and-center view of the lake. So, for now, maybe it could've been an owl I'd heard.

Or at least I hoped it was. Nothing was like it seemed anymore.

Celia continued forward and drew me into a hug. "It's good to see you." She pulled away, holding me at arm's length. "No demons, right? You didn't see anything?"

I tilted my head. "That's right."

"Then why do I smell your magic?" Her nose crinkled and she knitted her brow. "And why does it smell angry?"

I flipped back my hair. "Nothing to worry about. A new vamp decided he wanted to have a taste. I decided I didn't want to let him."

All it took was a look from Misha and the vamps lounging near us righted themselves and swooshed past me. Within seconds, one of the kinkier ones dressed like a naughty Catholic schoolgirl returned, dragging the vamp in question by the foot and dropping him directly in front of Celia.

"Here you go, Master. Tootles." She gave a little pinky wave and bounced away in a wild pair of killer leopard stilettos. For all I grumbled about the naughty Catholics, they had excellent taste in footwear.

Once more, Celia's tigress eyes returned to the surface. "This him?" she asked me.

At my nod, she yanked him to his feet by the collar and hissed. She wasn't as hostile as Tim, but I could still sense the rage. The vamp hissed back. He wasn't afraid of Celia. But he should have been. And *shit* was he ever scared of Misha.

The vamp's glare lessened in severity as he caught Misha stalking forward. Trembles racked his body hard enough to rattle his withdrawing fangs with each of his master's encroaching steps.

"Kitten," Misha said to Celia. "Take some time to entertain your sister. I will see to young Sal's discipline."

I held up a hand. "Misha, it's not a big deal. It won't happen again."

Misha regarded him carefully. "You are correct. It most certainly won't happen again."

Whatever she sensed in Misha's features made Celia loosen her hold. The vamp slumped to his knees, bowing before his master. Celia stepped past him to place her arm around me. "Come on. Let's head to the guesthouse."

Celia encouraged me to hurry with a firm press to my lower back. We stepped through the doors leading out to the terrace. She took my purse, allowing me to shrug back into my coat when a strong gust of wind blew snow from the morning's dusting across the flat stone and around my boots. Once outside she continued to rush us ahead, down the steps and through the path leading into the garden.

"So, what's Count Hotness going to do to him?"

A bloodcurdling scream had me whipping back toward the house and stirred flickers of lightning to zap from my nails. *"That,"* Celia answered. She shook her head, continuing forward. "I was hoping we'd make it to the house before he killed him."

"Misha killed Sal for trying to get a taste of me? In all fairness, I can't blame the poor bastard for wanting a bite. I'm like a tall glass of O positive to your peeps."

She shook her head. "Misha killed him for disobeying. We—you, me, Emme, and Shayna—are off limits. He's made that more than clear, I assure you."

I reached for the handle of my purse when she offered it. "But he didn't even know who I was."

"It doesn't matter. He should have asked. Taran, this whole

crap with the Tribe has raised the danger factor and fueled paranoia. No one's safe. You could've been a threat to Misha, or his family. In failing to question you, he could have put the entire compound at risk."

"So, he deserves to like, re-die? No time-out—no going to bed without a flaming redhead with big jugs?"

Celia's expression split between darkness and sadness. "This is their way, Taran. I don't condone many things that go on here. But there are practices and beliefs among the undead that have remained in place since the dawn of time. Insubordination could potentially lead to human fatality—"

"Or Misha's ass in a sling."

She shrugged. "That, too. Which is why discipline usually results in death, and why the exterior grounds will be watched until Misha is satisfied that no threat exists."

"All right, I get it." I gathered the collar of my coat around me when another gust of wind blew through the pines. I did sort of understand where the blood squad was coming from, and if I were one of them, maybe I wouldn't have been as skeeved. But I wasn't a vamp, so yeah, I was pretty creeped out. "Seems like a real cozy place to live, Ceel."

Celia stared ahead, offering me a weak smile. "It's not usually this violent. The vampires feed away from me, and Misha's family is so devoted to him, he rarely needs to enforce the rules." She prowled ahead. "But like I said, thanks to the war, nothing's like it once was. It's just what it needs to be."

As the trees thinned, I caught sight of the guesthouse and the sprawling view of Tahoe. "Home sweet home, then?"

She didn't bother to smile when she answered. "Misha has gone out of his way to make me feel welcome, yet despite his kindness and good intentions, this will never be my home."

"Then why do you stay?" I asked.

"Because for good or for bad it's my new life, and one I willingly chose. I know it's hard for you to understand," she added when she caught my frown. "But I'm trying to embrace it for all the good I can do and see it as a gift to help others."

Celia meant what she said yet the sadness in her voice was as palpable as the snow the wind brushed from overhanging pine branches. Regardless of her intentions, we both knew if Aric hadn't left her, no way would she be here with Misha.

"I wish things could be different," I told her. I meant that. I was close to all my sisters, but Celia was my best friend. Nothing was the same since she'd moved out. It was as if there was a piece of me missing. But damn, I still had Shayna and Emme. Celia had Agnes Concepción, Edith Anne, Liz, and Maria—the vamps who dressed like naughty schoolgirls and rarely wore panties.

She pushed open the door to the guesthouse and stepped through.

I quirked a brow. "You don't lock your door?"

My comment made her laugh. "I have vamps capable of filleting beings with their fangs guarding the grounds. Trust me, they're more effective than a deadbolt." She kicked her old canvas sneakers off while I stomped my leather boots clean.

Celia's inner kitty made her metabolism ridiculously fast and kept her warm despite the frigid temperature. But even she had her limits. For crying out loud, she was only wearing a tank top.

She crossed the kitchen and into the small family room, slumping onto the couch perched directly in front of the fireplace. I placed my coat on a hook by the door and sat beside her. "So," she said. "To what do I owe the pleasure?"

I didn't realize how upset I was until I spit the words out. "Gem and I had a fight."

She pulled out the hair band that was barely containing her long curls. They spilled over her shoulders in a cascade of loose ringlets. "About what?"

"Well, he's hurt that I still don't want him to claim me and upset because I don't want to meet his parents."

"He wants to introduce you to his parents?"

"Yeah. He does," I admitted quietly. I lifted my head to find Celia staring back at me like I was too stupid to breathe. "What?"

She crossed her arms. "Is this the part where you expect me to feel sorry for you?"

Usually, I was the pissy one, so her reaction rekindled my anger. "What's your problem?"

Angry tears brimmed in her eyes. "No, Taran. What's *your* problem? Jeez, you can be so completely selfish. Here you sit, all upset because the guy who's madly in love with you—who treats you like angels dropped you in his arms—wants to commit to you forever."

"Celia—"

She pointed at me. "And not only that, but he's so proud to have you as his partner, he wants to show you off to his family."

"But—"

She stood then. "Do you know that I would do anything to have what you have? Do you know you're living my ultimate fantasy, but are too dense to appreciate it?"

My jaw dropped. I should have talked to Shayna and Emme rather than dumping this on Celia's lap. Although it was close to Thanksgiving, and Aric had cut her loose almost three months ago, the pain was as raw as the day he told her goodbye. She was right. I was pretty selfish.

"Sorry," I said, my voice cracking.

She gathered her long mane, holding it back and appearing to think things through. "I'm sorry, too. It's hard for me to be objective. And I shouldn't be shoving my problems onto you." She dropped her hands and lowered herself beside me. "But it doesn't mean I don't care, or that your situation is any less important."

I stared out the large picture window. Small flakes floated gently from the graying skies only to spin in the passing breeze.

"It's not that I don't love Gemini, or that he's not the best thing to ever walk into my life. It's just that . . ." I couldn't finish my thought. By that point, I was simply too embarrassed. Compared to what Celia was going through, my issues seemed so stupid.

"It's just what?" Celia asked. Her husky voice had softened. She didn't like fighting with me, either.

I gnawed on my bottom lip. "I don't want to get hurt," I blurted. "You know that this thing with him could crush me if it becomes too serious and it doesn't work out."

Her full lips formed a thin line. She knew what I meant because things hadn't worked out with Aric the way she's hoped. "It's already serious, Taran."

"Not as much as it could be," I admitted. "I haven't let him in all the way. My past—our past—I . . . the walls are up, and I prefer them that way." I don't look at her as I continue. "You told Aric *everything*—what you went through—what it did to you. He saw how it affected you, and he knew what it must have taken for you to let him in." I stopped right there because I knew I'd said too much.

"And he still walked away," she finished for me.

I glanced up in time to see her heart breaking. She might be facing me, but the distance in her expression told me she was remembering. "Yeah," I said.

"So, if you give yourself completely to him, it would hurt that much more if he left you."

I nodded because that was all I could do then, considering the agony in her voice. "What if he doesn't leave you?" she asked. "What if this is forever and you're giving up the opportunity to be happy?"

"Ceel, if life has taught me anything, it's that happiness can be ripped away in a second. Pain is raw, real, and can last forever."

Shayna would have argued that happiness could last

forever, too. But this was Celia. What happiness she'd managed was stolen from her even though she didn't deserve the loss. For a moment, we waited in silence, the crackling flames from the fire the only sound.

When she finally spoke, she managed a small smile. "Is there someone else?"

I tilted my head, surprised she'd even ask. "Of course not."

Her widening smile made it clear she was trying to make a point. "Do you want there to be?"

"No."

She hugged her knees and rested her chin against them. "Then let me ask you again, what's your problem? I get that you don't want to get hurt. I get that you're scared. But you have to give me a little more than that."

"I'm not ready for marriage," I added truthfully. My eyes stung when I caught the hurt that erased her smile. Maybe I shouldn't have said what I did, but I couldn't help it. "The claim, the bond it creates, in the end, it won't mean anything if he leaves me."

"Maybe not," she said slowly. "But I think you owe yourself, and him, that chance."

I locked stares with her. "This could end really badly, couldn't it?"

She bowed her head, taking a moment to gather herself. "It could, but maybe in your case it won't."

I swore and rubbed my eyes. "I wish I could go through with this claim, Ceel, but I'm afraid I can't."

"Then don't, Taran. If it feels this wrong, you're clearly not ready."

It did feel wrong, and scary, and—yeah, *scary*. "The thing is, I don't think I'll ever be ready," I admitted.

She tilted her head as she considered me. "Maybe. Maybe not," she said. "But I hope so, because I think a lot of good can come from it." She leaned in closer. "The one thing I'm sure of is that if that moment comes, you're going to know it, and you're going to own it."

"But if it doesn't come, where will that leave me and my wolf?"

"Still in love," she said, her resolve seconds from crumbling. She swiveled in the direction of the fireplace, watching the flames dance in the hearth. "Claim or not, your love will remain."

"I'm not so sure Gemini would agree."

She faced me then. "Taran, despite Gem's frustrations and the needs of his beasts, he would never force you to do anything." She watched me for a beat. "But at the very least, meet him halfway and allow him the honor of introducing you to his parents. What's the worst that could happen?"

Maybe she was right. Relationships were all about give and take. So that meant maybe I needed to give, at least when it came to his folks. I sighed. "Can I ask you something that will likely skewer your heart and roast it over the fiery pits of hell?"

She laughed despite herself. "After that setup, sure, why not?"

"If you could go back to the night Aric claimed you, would you change anything?" *Like kick him in the balls when he tried?*

Celia's devastated expression met mine, but she managed a small smile. "Not a damn thing," she said.

Celia and I talked over lunch. Although she'd likely eaten a full meal with Misha, my girl knew how to put it away. Most of our conversation turned to small talk, but it was the advice she gave me that I clung to. She wanted me to meet Gemini's parents. That much was clear. As I thought about how she looked in my rearview mirror as I pulled out of vamp camp, so physically strong but so emotion- ally shattered, I thought maybe girlfriend was kind of a masochist.

Loved sucked bear balls.

And Liam probably ate them.

Instead of heading back to Dollar Point, I cut left and toward the mountain. I needed to see Gemini and simply tell him I would . . . be honored—no, not *honored.* That I would *love*—great, there was that word again. That I'd meet his folks. There. That was all I had to say.

Now, if only God could kill me before I actually had to say it.

My loyal Subaru trekked up the winding mountain path until I reached the Den gates. This was the only way in, at least for me. The hundred-plus acres encompassing the property were surrounded by high walls and guarded more heavily than Misha's pad. I was allowed through without incident but was then forced to flip off the *were* guard when he muttered something to his buddy about me being "the vamp tramp's sister."

With a poof of blue and white, I waved my flaming finger as I drove off. "Eat fleas and die, Marmaduke!" I yelled. Was it the classiest thing I could have done? Probably not. But like I mentioned, don't mess with my family.

The thick pines cleared, and sprawling grounds capped with miles of white greeted me as I made my way to the rows of three-story lodges divided by a main road. I didn't like coming here. For the most part, the *were* students training to defend the earth, and those seeking asylum from the war, regarded Celia as some kind of evil slut trying to seduce their revered pure- blood. My sisters and I were "welcomed" only because Koda, Liam, and Gemini weren't pure. Each had a human parent, whereas Aric had descended from a line of *were*-only blood.

Barbara, Aric's fiancée, was one of the last few pures left. Barbara rubbed this in our faces. Barbara used her status to her advantage. Barbara was a douchebag from the planet Bitch.

I rolled to a stop in front of the main building in time to see the local coven of witches hurry down the steps, the cloaks covering their medieval gowns fluttering around their ankles as they shuffled past me. The meeting between the *weres* and the witches must have just finished.

Oh, goody. Our first interaction with the coven hadn't been friendly and ended with lots of bloodshed and the destruction of a dance club. The dance club was a total accident; the bloodshed wasn't. It was safe to say the broom humpers didn't like us. It was also safe to say that I didn't care.

I strolled past them and up the stacked stone steps. "Waddup, peeps?"

Most paused and exchanged glances. A few actually

scowled. Although I could stir flame and lightning, they would never consider me to be a true witch. Witches used talismans, staffs, or some other tacky costume jewelry to amplify whatever magic they were born with. They also relied on chants and words of power. I gathered my magic from the environment around me, by absorbing it like a sponge through my core. Many a wicked witch considered it "stealing" from the earth. Truthfully, I didn't know how I did it, but I definitely wouldn't have called it *stealing*. Maybe *borrowing* was a better word. Besides, I didn't keep it. When I was done, I simply released my magic back into the world.

I crossed into the foyer only to have another witch stomp in front of me, glaring and blocking my path. Her blatant animosity sparked a warning and stirred my magic. "Problem?" I asked her, smiling.

"I'm Genevieve's second," she said, like it was supposed to mean something.

"So?"

Oh, she didn't like that. Nuh-uh. Not one bit. "So, I suggest you show some respect, freak," she said, inching closer. "No one likes you, or your pathetic excuse for magic. Watch yourself or you will feel the wrath of my might."

"'You will feel the wrath of my might?'" I repeat. "Are you *trying* to sound like Thor—No, no, let me guess. *Game of Thrones* fan, right?" I kept my smile despite her darkening expression and the rush of power snaking around her. She was trying to intimidate me. But the Four Horseman would gallop over my cold dead corpse in parachute pants before I'd let her push me around.

"I'm supposed to cower, right?" I asked. "Bow at your feet and maybe borrow your broom to clean your room or something? Sweetheart, that's so not going to happen. You don't scare me, and neither do your sorority sisters." My voice tightened. "You want my respect, you need to leave asshole status behind and earn it. And if you ever threaten me again, you're the one who'll learn what *real* power is."

"Taran," a deep, rough voice called out to me.

Aric abandoned the group of young *weres* he was speaking to and prowled forward. Despite that he was a big boy and that my magic flared around *weres,* I hadn't even noticed him. Too much mojo in the house, I supposed.

He stepped between us, taking in how the stupid ditz in front of me and I continued to watch each other. "Try it," I told her, sensing her magic amplify with her growing anger.

"Settle down," Aric said, making it clear he didn't want any trouble.

I cracked my knuckles and charged my fingertips with lightning, making it clear I wouldn't back down if she started something. "You ain't the boss of me," I sang brightly.

He pinched the bridge of his nose, but then dropped his hand away and addressed Genevieve's second. "The meeting's over. Until next time?"

"You're excusing this?" She motioned to me. "This disrespect."

Aric didn't flinch. "No. I'm ignoring the fact that you approached her unprovoked, and that you threatened her with harm." It's then something shifted in his gaze. "As I said, until next time."

Aric had a way of growling without actually growling. The witch realized as much and stormed away. The remainder of the coven trailed behind her, not bothering to hide their frowns. "Don't let the door hit your broom or your ass," I called.

Aric crossed his arms. "Jesus, just let it go, Taran," he non-growl growled.

Like Gemini, Aric was tall and muscular, but I couldn't help noticing he had bulked up quite a bit since I'd last seen him. Still, that didn't mean he looked good. Thick stubble blackened his jaw. He hadn't bothered shaving, and dark circles shadowed his brown eyes. A heavy blue flannel shirt covered his chest, and wrinkled jeans ran the length of his legs. He'd thrown the clothes on without much thought or care to his appearance. That wasn't like him. Well, at least when he was with Celia.

Being the sympathetic gal, I was, I articulated my concern for his well-being. "Damn, Aric. You look like hell."

He chuckled. "Thanks, Taran. Gem's in my office, setting up the next meeting with Genevieve, the clan's head witch."

"Okay." I turned on my heel to head down the hall, but then stopped. "What's up with the dead bodies you found?"

He waited a beat, as if debating whether to tell me. "They were found devoured. Chunks of muscles ripped from their bodies in small bites—"

I held up my hand to stop him, and to keep the lunch Celia and I had shared down. "Got it, thanks." Small bites could only mean one nasty thing. "Demon infants found those humans?"

"More likely Tribe *weres* or vamps found them and offered them to the demons as food. In a way, it's good news."

Bile swirled in my belly and threatened to inch up my throat. "Tell me exactly how finding eaten, and mutilated body parts is a glass-half-full kind of thing. You *weres* are a twisted bunch, you know that?" I brushed off the *weres* passing by, who snarled. "Oh, muzzle it—you furries know I'm right."

Aric rubbed his jaw, trying to squelch his grin. He'd lived with us long enough to know I didn't mean any harm. "The way I see it, to risk being discovered and venture out so close to Alliance territory means these Tribesmen are few, and desperate to keep their numbers," he explained. "The bite marks had two distinct mouth shapes, which means only two demon children fed. That's a lot better than the horde we faced a few weeks back."

"The ones from your mission to Haiti?" I tightened my stance. "Or the ones who came after me and my sisters?"

Aric leaned back on his heels, his deep voice lowering

further. "Both. But closer to the swarm that took Emme, Shayna, and Celia."

The memory of that day enclosed the room around me all at once. I unbuttoned my coat and slipped it from my shoulders, feeling suffocated. Aric's nostrils flared. As I carefully draped the heavy wool over my arm, I realized that after spending the last few hours with Celia, traces of her scent must have latched onto my clothes.

He closed his eyes and released a breath before opening them slowly. "How is she?" he asked. For an alpha werewolf, he didn't seem very dominant then. His gaze softened to that of a tamed beast as he waited for my response.

Again, maybe I shouldn't have said what I did. But as I stated, I just wasn't good at keeping my mouth shut. "Considering how much she misses you, about as well as can be expected," I told him honestly.

He squared his stance. "I miss her, too, Taran, every minute of the day. Don't stand there assuming I don't."

I should have been more sensitive to his pain, but I could only sympathize with Celia. He did this to them, not her. "If you miss her so much, why don't you call her? And maybe step up, grow some balls, and tell your Elders to kiss your ass and mine."

Okay, maybe I could have been a little less harsh.

His expression wavered between fury and frustration. "Watch it, Taran."

"It's hard to watch what I say when I see my sister hurting as much as she is, Aric." I gave him the once-over. "And truth be told, you don't look any better."

I closed the distance between us, whispering low. "Call her. Just pick up the phone and let her know you're thinking of her."

"I *can't*," he ground out. "The situation I'm in becomes more challenging if I see her or talk to her."

"Or kiss her?" For all that Aric felt compelled to stay away from Celia and fulfill his pureblood duties, he and Ceel had made out like horny teens at Koda and Shayna's wedding. And yeah, he'd instigated that one. "Aric," I said quietly, unable to keep the bite from my tone, "she loves you. You can't just let things end like this, especially when you're both so miserable apart."

"Taran, don't you think I hate what I did to her, and what I did to us?" he growled. "It kills me to know how much I hurt her. If there were a way out, I'd take it. But there's not. So, I live with my choice and hope like hell one day she'll forgive me, even though I don't think I deserve it."

He stomped away from me then. As furious as I was with Aric for hurting Celia, I wasn't completely made of stone. In breaking her heart, it was clear he had shattered his own.

I groaned. Maybe I shouldn't have told him to call her, knowing that if he did, it would affect them both. But there was a part of me that hoped they could somehow find a way back to each other. That wouldn't happen if he kept his distance, though I was sure Celia would keep hers. No, for something to happen, Aric would have to be the one to come through.

I swept down the dark-paneled hall and toward Aric's office in my quest to find Gemini, making enough noise between my swear words and stiletto stomps to wake the dead and probably most of China. Gem's head lifted when I stormed in, his attention leaving the laptop perched in front of him. He sat behind Aric's prim mahogany desk, surprising me with a warm smile. And although his alluring welcome heated me down to my toes, I couldn't return it.

I ground to a halt. Head witch Genevieve was standing way too close to my wolf, the bodice of her crushed-velvet emerald gown threatening to choke the breasts hovering inches from Gem's face. It was bad enough to find her standing so close. But her blatant flirting crossed a line.

She straightened at my arrival, albeit slowly, her fingertips leaving the strands of her ebony hair to brush against the large yellow stone anchored to her talisman.

If she meant it as a warning, she was threatening the wrong gal.

Gemini seemed oblivious to her advances, but I certainly wasn't. My eyes remained trained on her sapphire irises even when Gem pushed away from the desk and walked around to greet me.

Her hair might have been as dark as mine, but she didn't share my olive skin tone. Instead, ethereal fair skin covered her perfect heart-shaped face, contrasting boldly against her midnight brows and lashes. She wasn't beautiful. Nope. Tahoe's head witch was *gorgeous*.

Yet that didn't make her less of an asshole.

Gem slowed his pace as my flames snapped, crackled, and popped above me. He glanced back over his shoulder. "This is Taran Wird," he told her. "Taran, this is—"

"We've met," we answered. Her tone was lovely. Mine bordered on deadly.

My wolf knew the story but skittered around it. "At another time and under different circumstances," he said.

She abandoned her spot behind the desk, moving like silk as tendrils of bright yellow light swirled from her talisman to ribbon around her. "And under a different charge." Despite her words and light tone, she was raring for a fight.

Well, so was I.

I rounded on her. "You may not have been behind my sister's torture session, but you were part of the coven that was."

"It's a new coven, I assure you."

I shook my head. "No . . . same balls, different prick."

"Taran," Gem warned.

Genevieve smiled. "Are you calling *me* a prick?"

I edged around Gem when he stepped in front of me. "Yup.

And I'm calling you out for what your stupid friends did to my sister."

Blue and white light crashed against yellow. The room rumbled. I don't know what happened to Gemini; I only remember how heavy my legs felt as I forced my flaming body toward Genevieve. She squinted, trying to shield herself from the light, shoving her glowing body forward. I grunted as I felt my flames dwindle, calling them back, knowing she meant to silence me.

But hell hath no fury like a hot bitch like me. With a hard shove forward, and an even harder scream, my magic blew up and out, forcing her to stagger. Sparks peppered the room, like sharp steel blades rabidly meeting metal. I stumbled when the floor beneath us rattled and the lights above us flickered, but I stomped forward, ignoring the pain burning its way into my muscles.

From what seemed like the top of a mountain, Gemini growled my name, and something else. But I wouldn't respond, too busy concentrating on making my point: Bitch, keep your coven away from my family *and* your boobs off my wolf.

Every hair on my body stood on end as Vieve responded in turn, thrusting forward with a rush of power.

I thrust back, stubbornness and anger fueling my strength.

"Forze, solidita, vigore," she chanted.

Her surging magic slapped and heated my skin. I gritted my teeth. "Back off, Glinda. He's *mine*." I used my jealousy to charge her with an extra boost of fire.

For a moment, I caught a hint of surprise, before her surprisingly controlled demeanor splintered, revealing a touch of her rage. *"Potere, potenza, spiccato!"* she hissed, clutching her talisman.

"What the hell?" Aric growled from behind me.

I hurtled myself forward, in spite of my lead-heavy feet.

Vieve gasped, spitting out power words in Italian for all she was worth. My power words only contained four letters, but they seemed stronger than hers.

We were almost to each other. I reared my arm out, ready to punch her in her perfect face, when another magical presence pimp-slapped back.

I knew it was Makawee even before she touched our arms; her power as the pack omega as recognizable as the back of my hand.

"Ladies, *please*." Her voice was gentle, unlike the force she used to rip us apart.

My back smacked against the wall. Genevieve struck the far bookshelf, knocking over several bound novels. I tried to catch my breath, my attention skimming the area.

Oh . . .

Gemini and Aric loomed close by, their breaths ragged and their clothes singed, covered in blue, white, and yellow soot, the same soot coating every square inch of the once prestigious office.

They must have tried to separate us.

Oops.

Makawee's long white hair hung loosely behind her as she folded her hands in front of her body. She kept her voice soft and her body between us. "My," she said quietly, as if Vieve and I had merely exchanged insults. "It would seem all the Wird girls are a spirited bunch."

"Don't you mean Weird girls, Makawee?" Barbara offered.

Aric's fiancée had arrived. Oh goody. She shoved away from the doorframe and inched in my direction. Instead of screaming at her like she probably expected me to, I gave her a huge grin. "Is that where you keep your wolf!" I said with forced glee. She cocked her head. "Rammed up your ass," I clarified.

Gemini and Aric both groaned. Makawee tried to suppress a smile but didn't quite manage. She always did enjoy a good guffaw. Genevieve, though, caught me by surprise. She laughed, as in, like, totally and genuinely giggled at Barbara's expense.

She brushed off the magical dust coating her and walked forward, stopping a few feet in front of me. "It was good to see you again, Taran. Until next time?"

I returned her smile with one of my own, except mine wasn't as sweet. "Looking forward to it, Vieve."

Makawee merely shook her head and chuckled, joining Genevieve on her way out.

I watched the hem of Vieve's long dress disappear around the corner but kept my guard up. With Bridezilla this close, chances were my supernatural smack-downs were far from over.

Barbara hated Celia, and as her sister hated me, too. Well, can't say I got the warm and fuzzies around her, either.

She narrowed her eyes at me. I answered her with a wicked smile, and maybe a little flame as I strutted to Gem's side.

He stood ramrod straight. His stance and hardening expression told me he was majorly pissed. As much as it upset me to see him angry, I was more concerned that I may have injured him with my power.

My hands swept over his shoulders, in a half-assed attempt to brush off the soot. Um, yeah. That didn't work. If anything, all I managed was to drift poufs of soot into the air making us cough. I gave up and slapped my palms against my sides. "Sorry about the clothes, baby. Are you all right?"

"What are you doing here?" he asked slowly.

"He means besides causing trouble," Aric said when I didn't answer.

Aric's attempt at humor did nothing to ease the strain between me and my irate lupine. I knew Gemini was mad. But his tone, that of barely controlled rage, surprised me. I'll admit, maybe he had a right to be furious. That didn't mean his reaction didn't pain me.

"I came to see you."

I couldn't disguise the hurt in my voice or my face. But maybe it was what he needed to see and hear. His face softened and his demeanor slowly relaxed. He pulled me close, keeping his hands tight on my hips. "I'm sorry," he said quietly. "It's not that I'm not happy to see you. But what happened just now with you and Genevieve can't happen again. Am I clear?"

"She started it," I mumbled. Like I mentioned, I'm all kinds of mature.

Barbara stepped forward, and very close to Aric's personal space. Although her voice was low and seethed with enticement, she was plenty loud enough for me to hear. "You should ban her from our Den, Aric." She glanced back at me. "We can't risk her insulting our allies or creating another unwelcomed disturbance."

Her red nails matched her pouty lips. She ran them along Aric's arm, but didn't get far. He sidestepped from her reach. *His* voice? Now, that was far from enticing. "I'm not going to ban the woman who is both a valued member of our Alliance and the mate of my second in command."

I peered around Gem and motioned to Aric. "You forgot sister-in-law," I said, looking directly at Barbara. "He did claim my sister, after all."

Oh, and didn't I know how to bring the room to a grinding halt? Well, we all had our gifts. Barbara whirled on Aric, fast enough to whip her long blond hair behind her. "Is that true?"

Aric met her with equal force. "I told you, any discussion about Celia is off limits."

Barbara's scowl eased, replaced by a flicker of malice that caused both me and Gem to separate and edge closer to Aric. Her hand struck like a cobra, her nails clenching Aric's jaw so tight, droplets of blood trickled down her fingers. Gem lurched forward, growling, his response and Barbara's vindictiveness sparking my magic with fury. Aric lifted his hand, keeping us in place.

It was as if we weren't there, Barbara so intent in whatever asinine point she was trying to make, she kept her back to us. "It doesn't matter who was part of your past," she spat. "Like it or not, I'm the only future you'll know."

Two fingers. That was all Aric used to break Barbara's hold. He clamped them down on her wrist and removed her hand so forcibly, her nails peeled his skin away in chunks, leaving grisly lines that punctured deep into his skin.

Aric didn't growl. He didn't flinch. But that wolf was all rage. "I know my duties," he told her. "And I know my obligations. Don't think you'll ever be more to me than that."

He released her then. Barbara, while clearly stunned by his demonstration of force, clung to her wickedness and spite, refusing to let it go. She smiled with all the warmth of a gator. "My, what impressive strength you have, my love. Do you think our babies will inherit it?" Her smile widened as he straightened. "I can't wait to find out."

I'd seen a lot of carnage. But their interaction was hard to hear, to watch, and to take. Cruel. Barbara was simply cruel.

She walked away then, satisfied with the damaged she'd inflicted with her nails and her words, her hips swinging in that too tight dress. It was all I could do not to zap her for being so nasty.

Aric remained still as granite, lost in his thoughts, and hopelessly fated to someone with a soul cold enough to chill the Arctic. Blood dripped from his chin as his inner wolf sealed the goddamn holes on his face. *This* was the woman he'd left my sweet sister for, and the one he'd eventually breed with.

My voice quivered as I spoke. "I'll meet your parents."

"What?" Gem asked. He was so focused on Aric, and

keeping his wolf from going after Barbara, that he didn't register my words.

I faced him then. "I said I'll meet your parents."

He lifted my hand, but his expression remained solemn. "What changed your mind?" he asked.

"Celia did," I admitted. I squeezed his hand and glanced at Aric. "She said she'd give anything to have what we share."

Aric met my eyes with an expression so pained it stung me down to my toes. "So would I," he muttered.

He stormed out of the room then. In the opposite direction Barbara had disappeared.

6

---

glanced at the clock. "What's keeping her? Should I call her again?"

"Dude, relax. If Ceel said she was coming, she'll be here."

I whipped around to tell Shayna to try her again, only to get sprayed in the face with perfume. "Oops. Sorry, T," she said.

I coughed and gagged and would have glared had it not been for the perfume burning its way through my sclera and into my skull. I swore when I slammed my nose in the door-frame in my haste to reach the bathroom and rinse my eyes.

Emme clasped my elbow, leading me forward. "Here. Over here."

I nodded, turning myself over to Emme's gentle hold.

"Son of a *bitch*." I tripped over the small lip in the threshold, stumbled to my knees, and landed on something sharp. I rolled onto my side, agony ripping through me, only to have something poke me in the ass.

"Oh," Emme said when I yelped. "Don't worry, honey. I can fix that."

"Holy sharp stilettos, Batman," Shayna said from somewhere behind me. "You know, you shouldn't leave your shoes lying around like that."

"Get away from me before I kill you!" I screamed.

"Ah, maybe you should give Taran some space," Emme suggested, albeit from a good distance away.

I rose on my throbbing knees with my hands outstretched, trying to find my sink. Tears streamed down my face and snot poured out of my battered nose. Emme clasped my waist, angling my body, and positioning me against the sink. That was good. Until she blasted the cold water and drenched my bra and exposed skin. I jumped back from the frigid temperature and stumbled over my shoes—*again,* landing on my ass, *again.* For all the moaning Shayna did about leaving my shoes lying around, do you think cheerleader Barbie picked them up?

I smacked the hands away that were trying to help me up. "Don't touch me." My fire sizzled when either Emme or Shayna refused to let go. "I said *don't touch me!*"

I still couldn't see from the acid burn from the perfume. I rose slowly, and blindly made my way back to the sink. With every swear word I knew, I adjusted the water to less-than-freezing temps. I splashed my face repeatedly until the sizzle cooking my eyes lessened enough for me to see. I blinked back at my reflection. The hair I'd spent an hour straightening was ruined, clinging to my neck in wet clumps. Black lines cut across my face from the remains of the eye shadow, liner, and mascara I'd painstakingly applied. Snot continued to drip down my face and my nose was competing with the bright red swelling ringing my eyes. The eyes won.

Emme offered me a towel. I lifted it from her grasp and wiped my raw face. "Thanks—"

"Oh, wait, I think that one's dirty."

I slowly lowered it. She was right. I now had leftover whiskers from Gemini's goatee trim scattered across my face. It was all I could do not to beat my little sister to death.

Celia walked in then, her smile fading when she caught a good look at me. "Um. How's it going?"

"My tits are soaked, and I resemble Bozo the scary and hairy clown. How do you think it's going?" I snapped.

She moved toward me, tripping over my shoes and snapping the heel off one of the pairs I'd planned to wear. "Oh, sorry. You know you shouldn't leave those on the floor—"

"I know that!" I slumped over the sink and covered my face.

"Taran's having a rough few minutes," Emme explained.

Celia sighed and placed her hand on my shoulder. "Let Emme heal you. Jump in the shower, and let's start over." She looked to the ceiling when I belted out six swear words in a row. "Taran, Gemini's parents won't be here for another four hours. There's plenty of time to fix—well, everything."

My stinging eyes took in the mess on the floor and the mess that was me. I don't cry much. Things really have to be bad for me to shed more than a tear. But I wanted to then.

"I was going to make them dinner." I swallowed hard, trying not to lose it. "But I was worried I wouldn't have enough time to get ready." My body trembled with cold. I pushed back my wet hair, ready to cry for real. "I printed out all these recipes—food and appetizers they might like. How am I going to get everything done? It took me an hour and a half just to get ready."

Celia angled her chin. "This means a lot to you, doesn't it?"

"I just wanted to do something nice for them," I admitted. And I wanted them to like me. If not for me, for their son.

"Where are the recipes?" Celia asked.

I reached for a towel just to wrap myself with. "They're on the counter. By the coffee machine."

"We'll get started on them," she said. "Let Emme heal you. Get a shower and we'll take care of the rest. It's going to be fine, Taran."

I wasn't so sure. "Did you bring the dress?"

She smiled. "I did." I watched her disappear and return with a garment bag. She unzipped the bag, pulling out a long and elegant Asian-style dress. The blue satin, embossed with silver flowers, was the perfect color to compliment my eyes and skin.

I walked to her slowly, barely believing how stunning this dress was, as Emme and Shayna gushed over it. "Oh, my God," I whispered.

Celia laughed. "I know! It's one of a kind and exactly what you need to make a memorable first impression."

I lifted the bottom of the dress, examining it carefully. "Celia, how did you?—I mean, this is just, just . . . *awesome.*"

She laughed again. "Misha's name goes a long way. It arrived from Tokyo this morning from a designer he likely fed from. I sent her that picture you emailed me, told her your likes and dislikes, gave her your measurements, and she came up with this."

I threw my arms around her, believing for the first time that maybe she was right. Maybe I'd make a good impression after all . . .

I TOOK my time getting ready and did my best to relax. Although I'd planned to help in the kitchen, everything was done by the time I stepped out.

My sisters rushed over. "Taran, you look beautiful," Emme said.

"No, she doesn't, she looks hot," Shayna said with a smack to my ass.

I hugged Celia when she smiled softly. Although I didn't want to get all girly, it was hard then. She, like Emme and Shayna, knew how important this day was for me. "Thank you," I whispered. "I . . . just thank you."

"You're welcome, Taran," she said quietly.

I let out a breath when I pulled away, trying not to lose it again. "How much do I owe you for the dress?"

"Nothing."

I frowned. "Come on, Ceel. I can't let you pay for this."

"Consider it a gift," she said, motioning to Emme and Shayna. "From all of us."

So much for not getting girly. I hugged them tight when they gathered around me. More than once I'd wondered what I'd do without them. God willing, I would never find out. "Thank you," I told them, my voice cracking as I struggled not to cry.

"It's going to be okay, Taran," Emme said.

"You've got this, T," Shayna agreed.

I hope so. I released them carefully and walked into the kitchen, snagging the apron draped over the counter. "What needs to be done?"

"Nothing, we got you covered, T—oh, except for the fried tofu with peanuts. It will need to bake for a few minutes and then be topped with sprouts and the sauce."

"You can put it in while you're adding the shrimp to the baked toast," Celia added.

I was almost too stunned to speak. "Wow. You girls totally went above and beyond—" My head jerked when I remembered something. "I forgot the sake."

"What?" Emme asked.

I untied my apron and tossed it aside. "Gem mentioned how his father and mother enjoy this particular and rare kind of sake. It's expensive and hard to find, but I called a spirits shop in South Tahoe and the owner hooked me up. He ordered it from an upscale restaurant in Japan and had it shipped to his store." For the almost three-grand price tag and an additional handling fee, I didn't add. "It's at his shop. I meant to pick it up yesterday when I hit the grocery store, but I forgot."

Shayna skipped (because that's how girlfriend rolls) to the coat closet. "Here. I'll go. Come on, Emme."

"No. That's okay." It wasn't that I wouldn't trust those two with my life—because I would. I just wouldn't trust them with my sake. After their "help" in my room, I was worried they'd drop the bottle. "You've already done enough."

"It's really not a problem," Emme said. "We're happy to help."

There was that word again. I spoke through a tight smile. "Really, it's okay. I got it."

Ceel tried to suppress her grin, likely scenting my lack of faith in our girls just then. "Taran probably needs a distraction to help her relax. Why don't we stay and tidy up, so she'll be all set when Gem's folks arrive?"

Celia's reasoning was the something shiny they needed. I grabbed my keys and off I went.

Little did I know I was in for a lot more than I'd bargained for.

7

Bastard ghetto liquor store.

It was bad enough it was on the shoddier side of South Tahoe. But then the owner had to behave like a little prick. He placed the dark glass bottle in front me like some grand prize and smiled. "You're in for quite a treat, beautiful," he said. "This is a rare find—"

"Save it for someone who'll believe your crap."

He loomed over me, using the full bulk of his three-hundred-pound-plus body to try to intimidate me. Have I mentioned I don't intimidate easily? "What did you say to me?"

"Oh, I'm sorry. Did I stutter?" I jutted my chin and glared back at him. "I said you're full of crap, and so was your mother." I pointed at the bottle. "That's some cheap knockoff that goes for fifty bucks at any store. *My* sake—the one I'd paid close to three grand for—and the one you swore you'd have for me— doesn't look anything like this. So, give me what I came for before you really piss me off, dickhead."

"And what happens if I piss you off?"

It was then that I sensed it, and my vision sharpened. This shop owner wasn't human. He was something else.

Well, so was I.

I flung a finger out, sending a bolt of lightning to strike the closest bottle of vodka. It exploded in a wash of blue and white. "*That,*" I told the stupefied idiot.

He flung himself over the counter with a fire extinguisher. I leaned on the counter and drummed my carefully manicured nails. He growled over his shoulder. "*What are you?*"

I stopped drumming and straightened. "I'm the mistress of flame and light, the goddess of lightning, and the princess of fire. In other words, asshole, the woman who'll burn your store to ash if you don't give me my sake!"

For all he snarled and bared his teeth, he stood still. "The hell?" he said.

I thought he meant me, but his full attention was toward the open door behind the counter leading to a storage area. Cases of beer and booze were stacked along the back wall. The room didn't seem large, but I couldn't guess its size from where I stood.

I thought he meant to distract me so he could attack, until something stirred from within the dark room. The *were*—I'm guessing that's what he was—stilled, and paled.

I inched back slightly, trying to keep an eye on both him and whatever lurked in the darkness. "What was that?" I asked.

Flap. Flap.

No . . . not that. Not now.

"What is that?" I asked, this time a little louder.

"Nothing good," he muttered.

I pushed away from the counter, that eerie sensation I'd felt one too many times slapping my skin like a cold ocean wave. The *were* carefully lowered the extinguisher. I thought he'd crouch low and stalk forward, poised to attack—like any other self-respecting guardian of the earth.

Instead he took a cautious step back, then another, and headed for the exit.

For a supposedly lethal predator, this guy was a total chicken shit. "Nothing good?" I repeated, dumbstruck he was leaving. He nodded, but that was about it, edging further away from me. "Wait—where you going? Start howling and *call* your pack—"

Something with wings shot through the open door, quickly followed by another something. I dove to the floor in time to see a demon child the size of a raccoon latch onto the *were*'s face and begin to feast—as in *eat his face* . . . three seconds before a smaller version landed between my outstretched legs and hissed.

"Holy *God*!"

There was no grace to my reaction, no strategy.

Screw grace and strategy, I wanted to live, damn it.

Blue and white flames fired from my fingertips, igniting a wing. The little freak flew off with a screech, spiraling in circles as he attempted to fly with one wing. He crashed into a Budweiser display, lighting the cardboard cutout of a model with giant grin on her face.

I scrambled to my feet, keeping my back against the wall, my eyes darting in all directions and my heart thumping hard against my chest. With a nausea-inducing rip, the *were* tore the famished demon from his face, severing a huge lump of his skin in the process.

The creature landed before me, greedily swallowing the remains of what resembled a nose. The *were* fell back screaming, a fountain of blood spurting through his hands. But I didn't care about the shop owner. Not then. The demon child in front of me had my full attention.

I zapped it with a mini lightning bolt, and another, and another, and—crap—another after that. He skipped away from each blast, stopping to stare at the singe marks I'd left only to flicker his forked tongue . . . no, make that flicker his *tongues* my way. The little turd had three of them because clearly, he wasn't creepy enough with one.

"You won't touch me," I told him through clenched teeth.

He laughed, his tongues slapping and sliding through a row of bloody fangs and his balls swinging in the breeze like Christmas bells. He crouched on his hind legs, his reptilian tail flicking excitedly and a hunger lighting his beady red eyes. I lashed out, firing white and blue light as fast as I could. He leapt away from every strike, appearing to enjoy my mounting terror and baiting me into exhaustion.

Jesus. The best way to describe this thing was an erect cat skinned of its fur. Strange markings ran along his belly and dwarf limbs. He wasn't as large as the ones that had taken my sisters, but these things caused chills to puncture my heart—not just because of what they looked like, but because of what they were. Demon children were bred from demon lords and very unwilling human women.

I shoved my fear away and focused. Hell would host the Ice Capades before I'd become his next prey.

The *were* continued screaming, because yeah, no help coming from that corner. I watched, waiting, building my magic between breaths and releasing blast after blast. The demon evaded each one. He thought he was smart.

But I was smarter.

I aimed, taking out another bottle of vodka. The demon laughed when I shot a bottle of bourbon and a supersized bottle of Jack after that. He thought I'd missed, until he glanced down at the booze soaking his feet.

I released my flame at the puddles of alcohol surrounding his form. A crest of blue and white engulfed him, my cue to scramble to my feet and fling myself over the counter. I landed on my heels—no way was I ruining my dress—in time to hear the thing shriek, and for wet entrails to splatter against the wall like confetti. Pieces of demon slithered down, thankfully drying in the air as he reached the warped floorboards.

Another holler from the store owner, another screech. I stumbled to a stand and peeked over the counter. The other demon child, the one I'd first injured, was taking his turn on the store owner's face. I should have been grossed out—it was all sorts of sick. But I was more annoyed than anything. "Rip off its wings!"

He screamed louder, causing me to yell. "Rip off his wings—his *wings*!"

The owner gurgled and choked, but managed a "*What?*"

I cupped my hands. "Rip off his wings and throw him in the fire." I pointed wildly for all the good it did me. "The *fire!*" I hollered.

His screams morphed into choked bubbling. "Oh, for heaven's sake." I stomped over, lifted the fire extinguisher, and zapped the bastard—the demon, I mean, not the giant prick getting his face chewed off.

The demon rolled off the store owner and I smashed him in the head with the extinguisher. I took about two steps back and finished singeing the little bugger. Although the smoke detector blasted above us, the exploding demon innards were moist enough to put out the dwindling flames.

That said, *ew.*

Repulsion, and the experience, might have made me a little irritable at that moment. Just a little bit. "What are you, deaf?" I snapped at the owner. "I told you to rip his wings off and toss him in the fire—"

The store owner sat up then. Blood soaked his face, shirt, and the sides of his head where the demons had eaten his . . . ears.

"My bad," I told him.

I placed my hand over my belly, mostly because I was trying not to puke, and eased back to where I'd dropped my purse. I rummaged through it, swearing when I realized I'd forgotten my phone. "Where's your phone?" I asked.

"Huh?"

"You're phone!" I screamed. "I need to borrow your phone!"

He wiped his face with his nasty shirt and pointed. "You calling the *weres*?"

I wanted to. But I couldn't. Not today. My fingers dialed quickly, although they were shaking more than I liked. Call me a coward, call me a wussy, call me a priss, but demons just plain suck.

"Who is this?" Tim hissed on the line.

"Cleanup in aisle nine," I told him.

"Taran?" he asked. "What's with you? Your voice is shaking like you've seen a ghost."

"No. Not a ghost." It didn't take a genius to figure out things were all sorts of effed up. Fear, and the adrenaline pumping through me, racked my body and found their way into each syllable I spoke.

"What happened?" Tim barked. "And, where are you?"

"I'm at Big MoFo Beers in South Tahoe. You know how Misha feels like he owes us? Well, I'm calling in a favor . . ."

I HAD my bottle of sake—the real one the owner had tucked beneath the register. It wasn't like he told me where he'd stashed it. If it hadn't been enclosed in the shiny red box, I probably wouldn't have found it.

I was contemplating taking a shot of Captain Morgan when Misha stalked in, flanked by his walking dead peeps. They took in the damage around them, their expensive shoes crunching over the sea of shattered glass.

Yeah, you might say I knew how to bust things up.

Tim's eyes cut to Misha. "I don't smell them, Master," he said.

Misha knelt in his fine tailored gray suit where the fire had roasted the demons. He took a whiff, grimacing when something reached his nose. "Did you burn them with alcohol?" he asked me. At my nod, he turned to his vamps. "Alcohol cleanses the air of iniquity. What remains should dissipate by the hour."

"But, Master, how could they survive this close to the lake's purity?"

Misha shook his head. "I don't know. Tahoe's power should have sickened them or forced them away. But we remain a good distance from its shore, and the building's brick exterior likely shielded them to some extent." He scanned the surroundings. "Regardless, their time here would have been brief."

Okay. He had my attention then. "So, you're thinking they were hunting outside the perimeter and ventured in?"

"That's probable," Misha agreed, rising with ease. "The lake's power, even on creatures as vile as this, is strong enough to repel them."

He regarded me then in a way that demonstrated he was taking in more than my dress. "Why didn't you contact Celia or your wolf? And why did you ask me to keep the incident and your whereabouts from her?"

I thought about what awaited me. Maybe supernatural smack-downs weren't so bad after all. "Today's a special day, and I don't want to screw it up."

"Does it involve your wolf?"

"Yes." We weren't exactly chummy, but I couldn't lie to Misha even if I wanted to. These supernatural senses could be downright annoying. "Look. His family is visiting. It's kind of a big deal. Could you figure out what happened on behalf of the Alliance? I'll fill Gemini in later."

"And your sister? I fear she will be angry at me for keeping this from her."

That's what he claimed, but I didn't miss the wicked grin that followed. I wasn't sure what he was up to; he probably wanted something in return. But no way would I be stupid enough to owe a master vamp a favor. "Then tell her. It could be one of many sweet little secrets you share. Just wait until she gets back to your place," I added quickly, and rather testily.

He quirked an eyebrow. Perhaps I'd spoiled his fun, and perhaps I didn't care. "Very well," he said.

"Thanks, Misha." I clutched my sake close, and walked to where the store owner had found a corner to lurk in. I bent to see how he was. What can I say? I'm a hell of a gal. "You okay?" I asked. For all that he'd been a jerk, he didn't deserve to be chomped on like steak.

He'd stopped bleeding, but that was about all I could say. "I asked if you were okay," I repeated, louder.

"They'll grow back!" he yelled. He stood, watching me. "Who are you, anyway? You're kind of badass."

"No one," I said. I didn't want to admit I was the girlfriend of Aric's second in command, especially if I wanted to keep this incident quiet a little longer. Thing was, for a local *were,* he should have known at least something about me, or at least my sisters in general. Maybe he was new. *Weres* seeking asylum had migrated to Tahoe in droves.

"How about dinner sometime?" he asked, patting my ass.

I stepped away from him and I swear, it took all I had not to smack him. Not only had he tried to dupe me out of my sake, taking my hard-earned money, and behaved like an overall asshole, but he lay like a bleeding slug while I took on two demon children by myself—and now he copped a feel. "I don't date conniving assholes who try to take advantage of a desperate damsel in distress," was my response.

Well, I didn't.

I stomped away then, muttering obscenities. Oddly enough, the stress of my day was far from over.

8

I reached for the bag of baked treats I'd bought on my way out of South Tahoe so it wouldn't spill when I made the turn into my development. Despite the day I'd had, I smiled when I glanced at the clock. Thirty minutes. I still had time left to unwind—more if the flight Gem's parents had taken was delayed.

I willed myself to relax. *No demons,* I reminded myself. *No death. No missing body parts.*

It's all good. All good.

Until it wasn't.

Mrs. Mancuso was placing a Christmas garland around "Carl," her freaky lawn jockey with the lazy eye. Come on. We still had two weeks until Thanksgiving. Besides, this woman was more Scrooge than Jolly Saint Nick.

I pulled into my driveway, steeling myself for what was coming and praying to sweet baby Jesus in the manger that for once she'd ignore me, for once she'd keep her trap shut, for once she'd walk back into her house.

Well, sweet baby Jesus must have been busy making the blind see or tending to some poor sap with leprosy. No sooner did I step out of my car with my bags tucked under my arms than she attacked. The malevolent bag of bones in support hose appeared like smoke right in front of me. She laid into me like she'd been lurking in the bushes with Carl, waiting for my arrival. "Dressed like a tramp as always, I see," she whispered.

Today was not the day to piss me off. Demon children and bloody shop owners with missing ears aside, I still had Gemini's parents to meet and greet.

I stomped away, or at least I tried. But I was in heels, and, well, Mancuso was like an Olympic sprinter in those orthopedic shoes she wore. She swept in front of me. "Tell me, does the Whore of Babylon know you took her clothes?" she asked. "Or do you find her attire too conservative for your slutty tastes?"

She eyed me then, very much like vultures eye a carcass before their first bite. "In my day, women dressed like ladies," she sneered. "Not harlots the likes of you or your trashy sisters."

It took all I had not to throw my bags at her. "Goddamnit, woman. Why are you here? What do you want? And *what's* your problem?"

"You," she said in a low voice. "You and your horrible family have completely soiled this neighborhood. You're nothing but sinners deserving of a public stoning."

Okay, I was pissed—furious even. Yet a smile spread across my face when I realized Mancuso and I were all alone. No Shayna to pull me back in the house. No Emme begging me to ignore her. I'd been waiting for this moment for a long time and considering my last few hours—and the fact that she'd had to go and put down my family—I wasn't holding back. "You know what? You are the biggest pain in the ass this side of Tahoe...,"

"Taran," Celia called from the door.

I continued, ignoring her. "I can't wait until you die. . ."

"Taran!" Celia beckoned louder.

"... and when you do," I said, narrowing my eyes, "I swear to God I will run up and down the street naked ..."

"Taran, stop it!" Celia raced forward.

"... singing, 'Ding-dong, the witch is dead!'" I snapped.

"Taran!"

"So, take your sagging neck skin, flip it over your shoulder, and get away from me, you wretched old c—"

Celia covered my mouth, her eyes wild and her expression one of sheer horror. "Taran," she whispered frantically. "Gemini's parents are inside."

The color drained from my face and down to my ass. "Wh-what?" I stammered.

Celia dropped her hand away from my mouth, stopping to glance back at the house and speaking low. "They took an earlier flight and arrived about ten minutes after you left—we tried calling you, but you left your phone on your nightstand."

"Where's their *car*?" I squeaked. I whipped around. Mine and Celia's were the only cars in the driveway.

"In the garage," she muttered. "We were, ah, trying to be nice."

I simply stared, *stared,* clutching my bags tight as if they could somehow shield me. This day couldn't possibly be real.

Mrs. Mancuso met me with a wide and enthusiastic grin. "Good luck meeting the folks," she said. She walked away then, with a skip to her step that I'd never seen.

It was all I could do not to smoke her ass.

Celia clutched my elbow to steady me. I took a breath, and then another, willing myself to remain vertical. "D-do you think ..." I tried to settle my nerves. Stupid nerves didn't let me, since they insisted we were screwed anyway. "Do you think they heard me?" I managed.

There was positively no flicker of hope anywhere in Celia's features. None. The last time I'd seen her look at me that way, she was paralyzed by magic and freaking demons were flying away with her. "Taran . . ." she began. "The whole neighborhood heard you. Mr. Fitzgerald across the street called Emme to ask what was going on with you and Mrs. Mancuso."

I couldn't move. Not even a little bit. Celia took my bags and led me into the house, my body trembling with total humiliation. I stepped through the door and into our large, open family room.

Gemini sat with his face buried in his hands. His parents waited on the couch, stone-faced, unmoving, their lips pursed tight as if they'd been sucking on lemons in my absence. Emme's jaw hung open while she held a tray of hors d'oeuvres in front of Gem's mom and dad. Shayna took one look at me and bolted into the kitchen. I watched her disappear, wishing I could join her.

I swallowed hard, my voice quivering. "Hello. I'm Taran. Did you have a nice flight?"

Gemini lifted lifted his head, defeat marching across his face like an army of Huns. I shrugged out of my coat, mostly because I didn't know what else to do then. His eyebrows drifted to his crown line when he saw me in my dress.

He stood and crossed the room to meet me, taking each of my hands into his. He smiled, the warmth in his dark almond eyes causing me to melt. "You look beautiful," he whispered, lifting my hands and kissing them softly.

I sighed, at both his presence at my side and his show of support. Maybe I stood a chance after all.

Maybe.

He released one hand but held tight to the other, leading me forward to where his parents remained unmoving on the couch. Slowly, they rose to their feet, their spines as rigid as metal poles and their irate expressions unflinching.

Gem bowed. "Father, Mother, I would like to introduce you to Taran, my mate. Taran, these are my most honorable parents, Zen and Aiko Hamamatsu."

The pride in his tone when he called me his mate brought a sting to my eyes that had nothing to do with the stupid perfume that assaulted me earlier. I hadn't expected to react this way and did my best to beat down the emotion.

Keep it together, girl.

I placed my hands on my lap to bow when they did. Emme was all about manners. She'd been Googling proper Japanese etiquette on my behalf for days and had me practice the night before. "I am very honored to make your acquaintance," I said. I erected my posture carefully, just like that lady had in the YouTube video Emme had showed me.

Gem appeared, like, totally impressed. His parents . . . not so much.

They ignored me and looked back at Gem. "Your mate does not seem to be aware that it is our custom to regard our elders with respect," Pop Hamamatsu said.

Gem dropped his eyes and bowed, while I did my best not to hurl. "I assure you, Father, Taran is extremely respectful of others," he said. "Especially those well into their years."

Momma Hamamatsu wasn't so convinced. She swiveled her head in my direction. "Then why did she speak so terribly to that frail woman?" Her pursed lips wrinkled further. "A kind woman who welcomed us so warmly."

"What?" I asked like a moron.

Gem's face flushed. "Gardening is one of my mother's favorite pastimes. She was admiring Mrs. Mancuso's elm." He squared his jaw. "Mrs. Mancuso made it a point to find out who they were and what they were doing here as she showed them around her yard."

I was going to fry Mrs. Mancuso to cinders. I knew it then. The old battle-axe had totally set me up. No wonder she'd whispered her insults.

I glanced over my shoulder at Celia. "Help me," I mouthed.

Her idea of "help" consisted of running for her life. "Ah, we should go and let you catch up," she offered. She grabbed Shayna, who was peering around the wall, and dragged her out of the house. Emme excused herself, placed the food on the coffee table, and charged after them.

Gem bowed again and attempted to explain my attack on that poor, defenseless elderly woman from hell. "Mrs. Mancuso is not fond of many," he said. "She often instigates quarrels—especially with Taran, forcing her to lose her patience. She's not the frail kind of woman she pretended to be."

Momma and Pop barely blinked. "Perhaps life has not been kind to her. More reason to show her sympathy and respect," Pop said. He turned back to me. "To injure an opponent with harsh words is to injure yourself."

If "life" hadn't been kind to Mancuso, it probably meant Mancuso had managed to piss "life" off, too. And what was up with the Yoda-ish?

Mancuso a pain is she.

Of course, that wasn't what I said. As upset as I was that I'd been made to look like the bad guy, I didn't need to add more fuel to the inferno I was currently standing in. What I needed was damage control.

I didn't have many options then. But I had sake.

"Excuse me." I hurried to where Celia had placed my bags on the small hall table, only to pause and turn back around when I remembered that I'd forgotten to bow. Son of a bitch. Being polite was exhausting. I reached for my liquor store bag and brought it over.

This time I remembered to bow but ditched the whole "honorable" mention. I pulled the sake out of the bag and handed it to Pop. "Here. I'm sorry. I meant to place it in a gift bag, but I didn't have time."

Momma nodded, although her features remained tight and unreadable. Pop admired the bottle enclosed in a beautiful box.

"Ancient Beauty," he said, sounding slightly awed despite his severe scowl. "Thank you for this fine treasure."

"Yes, thank you," Gemini said quietly. Although he seemed grateful, he probably hadn't liked me spending so much. I didn't have money to throw around, but I wanted to do something nice for his parents, and for my wolf. If that meant tossing a few grand to do so, I would do it and not think twice.

After Mancuso-gate, I'd probably have to shell out more.

I smiled, imitating Emme's subtle yet respectful grin. "You're very welcome. It pleases me to please you." I cringed. That sounded better in my head.

Gem angled his chin in my direction, the corners of his mouth lifting slightly. "Well done," he whispered.

I shook out my hands nervously. Okay. I was on a roll. I motioned to the other bag, hoping to keep up the momentum going. "In addition to the dinner my family helped me prepare, I brought some treats for dessert. Gemini—I mean, Tomo—mentioned you have a sweet tooth, honorable mother."

They bowed again, maintaining their stern expressions. Momma gave me her back and lifted a small gift bag with shimmering silver paper fanning out from the top. She bowed once more and offered it to me.

I put my hands up in protest. "Oh, no, I can't take this," I said. "I should be welcoming you."

They both frowned and pursed their lips as if I'd flashed them my breasts. Then again, maybe Pop would have liked that.

Gem leaned into me. "Ah, Taran. It's a Japanese custom to bring a gift to someone's home. It is an insult not to accept," he murmured.

Of course, it was. "I'm so sorry," I said, bowing like a maniac. "I didn't mean to disrespect you. Thank you—thank you so much."

I practically ripped the bag in my haste to retrieve the gift inside and demonstrate enthusiasm. I gasped when I unraveled the paper and saw what they'd brought me. A beautiful Japanese hair ornament meticulously embellished with a spray of white and silver flowers and added pearls took up my entire palm.

"It's lovely," I said. I combed it through the side of my hair and pushed it in place. "Thank you." I wasn't sure what it looked like on me. I was just happy my actions seemed to please them.

"Tomo told us that you have beautiful, long hair," Momma said. Although she'd given me a compliment, her face remained impassive.

I nodded and thanked her because I couldn't gather a better response.

"And our most gracious thanks for the sake and the sweet cakes," Pop added.

Neither would smile, but their kind words were a step forward. I smiled with my whole damn heart. "You're very welcome. I wanted to bring you something to welcome you into our home."

It was as if I'd snatched the sake out of their hands and cracked it open with my teeth. Gem's parents trained their scowls on him, but it was Pop who spoke. "Tomo," he said, gruffly. "What does your mate mean by 'our home'?"

And there was that monstrous step back.

9

———

The navigation system led us through a winter wonderland. Snow-covered pines linked their bending limbs to create beautiful archways that beckoned us and invited us through. Any other day, I would have leaned in close to Gemini as he drove, nibbled on his ear, and suggested he pull over to the nearest clearing for a romp in the snow.

Yet it wasn't just us.

And it wasn't romantic.

But it was rather memorable.

Except not in a good way.

To say I was losing altitude in the parent department would suggest I was still airborne. I'd doused myself with gaso- line and crashed in flames long before this. I should have paid closer attention to Japanese customs—and Gemini should have warned me that his parents didn't know we lived together.

"I wanted to wait to tell them in person," he'd said.

"Why?" I'd screamed afterward, my arms flailing wildly.

He rubbed his eyes. "So, they could meet you and better

appreciate my decision to live with you despite the fact that we're not officially mated."

I'd like to say that was all to it, but no. It had been the day from hell. In all the ass-kissing that followed my sisters' departure, I burned the food. All of it. Even the son-of-a-bitch tofu. So, my nice "dinner" consisted of sake and leftover bear organs.

That was bad enough. But it was all in the past, right?

Nope. Not even a little bit. I wouldn't be me without another humiliating hurrah.

Gemini's parents were actually quite the adventurers in their prime, and even well into their years. Before the start of the supernatural war, they spent three years climbing the highest mountains in Asia. But they'd never climbed anything in this country outside of Colorado, where they'd raised their son. "Dude take them climbing over the ravine," Shayna suggested. "Koda says a werecouger owns a place specifically for *weres* he runs year round."

I searched the website. The pics of the sprawling and magnificent views of the landscapes, along with the breathtaking images of colorful sunsets, convinced me this was a great idea—though I couldn't care less about mountain climbing. I recognized what a treat this could be for Gemini and his folks, and how it could possibly salvage what remained between us.

So, I saved all the best pics from the site on my phone and dropped another grand on this supposed adventure of a lifetime.

Although his folks weren't speaking to me, not that they were a chatty bunch, mind you, I offered them my phone so they could scroll through the pictures. I hoped the images would entice them—I mean, how could they not? The scenery was positively spellbinding.

At first, they remained quiet, appearing shockingly uninterested. Slowly, they started muttering in their language and pointing to the photos. For all their pursed lips and unyielding expressions, they seemed to warm then, their excitement appearing to build.

Until they went one back, to a selfie of me and Gemini.

In bed.

With my right breast exposed.

And their son sucking on the left.

Instead of leaning close to him, I sat on the passenger side as far away as I possibly could. I glanced his way. His hands remained tight on the wheel, his focus straight ahead, his face still bright red. Good God in heaven, it had been a long two days.

His gaze bounced to mine. "I'm sorry," I mouthed for the gazillionth time.

His face reddened further. He cleared his throat and said something in Japanese. For a human, his father had quite the bark. He said something I didn't understand, which reddened Gem's face further. He lowered his voice and said something more to his folks, his voice firm, yet bordering on pleading.

I rubbed my eyes. I didn't want to know what they said, knowing it wasn't good and that it involved me. But I had to ask. I couldn't have them mad at him. "What's going on?"

Gemini didn't answer me right away. "My parents are concerned about the events and feel perhaps it may be better if they return to their hotel suite."

"Oh, no. Please don't." I angled my body around to face them. Nothing but loathsome energy greeted me. Christ. It was like meeting Mrs. Mancuso's distant Japanese cousins. "I'm so sorry for anything you might have seen that depicted your son in a negative light. I assure you"—boobie flicking aside—"he's been nothing but a gentleman."

Their eyes narrowed further, and the lips puckered tighter. I was trying to kiss ass. I'll admit it. They probably saw right through it, his mom being a *were* and, both being well, all sorts of creepy. I opted for the truth, or at least something they could relate to. I motioned to Momma but spoke to Pop. "You're mates, right?"

"Taran," Gemini warned. "Perhaps it might be best to leave them to their thoughts."

In other words, *Zip it—my parents have already seen me suck on your large yet tantalizing nips.*

Maybe I would have listened to his underlying warning, but their exchange of nods and glances urged me on. "Well, then I'm sure you must have participated in your share of intimate moments."

"Taran," Gemini cautioned again, this time through clenched teeth.

Yikes. For someone who hadn't been attacked by demons as recently as I had, he was on edge. I threw out a hand. "Babe, my point is your parents have known need, and want, and desire." I angled around to face them. "Am I right?" Oddly enough, they didn't answer. "And I have no doubt it's been beautiful and memorable." I smiled, really smiled then. "And I love that for you. I hope you can find it in your hearts to love it for your son as well." My grin widened. Yeah, folks. You're welcome.

"From the very first moment I saw Aiko, my heart was lost," Pop said. "I could not find it, until I realized she held it with hers."

I placed my hand over my chest. "Oh. That's so sweet."

His face carried all the warmth of marble and so did his voice. "So, I did the proper thing. I surrendered to her hold. I took her as my bride. I welcomed the claim. All within days of our first encounter." He angled his head in her direction. "She was mine to respect and cherish. Never would I have treated her with anything less."

Well. I never had anyone tell me "fuck you" without using the actual words, but Pop did a banner job then. "Ah . . ."

Gemini swiped his brow. Oh, God. For all I thought *I* was

looking bad, I was making him appear worse. "Baby, I'm so sorry," I whispered.

Pop continued, laying into Gemini. "You call her your mate, Tomo," he said, not bothering to speak Japanese this time. "Yet you have not claimed her, choosing to use her to sate your own needs."

"Oh, but that's my fault," I stammered. "Lord knows he's wanted to claim me. I mean, *every* time we're alone—"

Their glares and Gemini's groan told me I should stop right there before Momma and Pop envisioned way past nipple suckage. So, I did.

I didn't need a shovel. I did fine burying myself deeper without one. "Jesus," I muttered.

The trees slowly thinned and opened into a large lot. Aside from two other SUVs, we were the only ones there. I couldn't slip out of the car fast enough, needing air and to fix everything I'd so far screwed up.

I wrenched open the rear side door as Momma tried to step out, causing her fall to the ground. Not to sound like an ass, but for a *were,* I expected better reflexes than that.

"Oh, *sh*—I mean, Oh, *no.* Are you okay, Momma?"

She rose easily enough, and while my name for her offered the barest pause, she didn't seem any happier with me.

Go figure.

Gemini and Pop hurried around the SUV, the sound of Momma's tiny body crashing against the frozen ground beckoning them to us. Their widening stares danced from her to me, regarding me like I'd shoved her. "Oh, my God. I'm so sorry. It won't happen again."

Pop led Momma a little farther from my reach. "Perhaps it would be best to return," he said.

"Please don't." It was one thing for them not to like me, but I hated them being angry at Gem. And in all fairness, while I might not be up for favorite girlfriend of the year, I hadn't had one decent shot. "Look. Let's take a walk. According to the website, there's a lookout." I stomped along in Shayna's hiking boots to the rear of the SUV and popped it open, retrieving the heavy backpack I'd brought. I hefted it and scrambled back to where they stood, speaking fast. "I brought food for lunch. Hot potato soup and bear liver sandwiches." I tried not to cringe. "You like bear liver, right?"

Gemini lifted the backpack from my shoulders when his parents did little more than blink back at me.

"Mother, Father, my mate is trying to please you. Please allow her this opportunity."

While they seemed to listen, they appeared far from convinced. I stepped forward. "We've come so far. At least let's make it out to the lookout and have lunch."

Pop turned to focus at the far end of the lot, where a stone and steel rope blockade had been erected to prevent cars from going over the ravine. Further out were more of Tahoe's magnificent slopes. My breath released in short bursts. The altitude was making it hard to breathe, especially considering how fast I was talking, but I was determined to make this a good day.

I took a few steps forward and motioned in the direction they were looking. The view was impressive, and we were just in the lot. I hoped they realized as much. "In the summer, the snow melts and all you see is green for miles. It's a different look, and while beautiful, not as spectacular as what you'll see today if you give it a chance." I shrugged, trying to sound more relaxed. "Between the war and all the demon activity that's been spotted in recent days, very few supernaturals venture out. We're probably the only tourist types here."

Again, they didn't speak. I tried not to swear, but it was hard. I wasn't one to beg, but I all but fell on my knees then. "This is a once-in-a-lifetime experience," I insisted. "I can't give you much, but please let me give you this memory." *And hopefully erase the one with my ankles fastened around your son's waist.*

Gemini stalked to my side. It was clear from his expression that he was humiliated, but I also saw a small speck of pride. He slipped his arm around my waist, holding me close. "Honorable Father and Mother, despite what you may feel, and the doubts that plague your mind, my mate only means to please you."

Momma and Pop considered me, very much the way feral dogs consider the rotting possum on the side of road—not too tasty, but necessary nonetheless. Both bowed in stone-faced and unimpressed unison. If I didn't know they were husband and wife, they'd make one freaky-ass set of twins.

"Very well, Tomo," Pop agreed.

A young man with strands of dirty-blond hair spilling from his beanie jogged over. "Hey, folks," he said. "I'm Lex." He sniffed and grinned. "Wolves?" At Gemini and Momma's nod, he turned to me, his smile widening. "And something else." His smile lessened at Gem's growl. "Ah, sorry, boss. But you can't blame a coug for looking."

"You're wrong. I can," Gem snarled back.

"Um, yeah. This way," he said.

I wasn't sure why Gem growled as ferociously as he did. I *was* "something else." Probably a tramp in his parents' world, but in his defense my poor wolf wasn't in the best mood.

"Shall we?" I asked, tilting my head where Lex was motioning. "A picnic, and maybe some climbing if you're up for it?"

"We make no promises," Pop said.

Gemini tossed the pack over his shoulder and linked his bare hand with my gloved one. Like Pop, I was dressed in full arctic wear since neither of us possessed the furry inner beasts of our partners. We started out at a fast walk, which Lex quickened to a trot.

For an old man, and a non-*were,* Pop kept pace behind us well enough. Gemini snaked his arm around me, helping me maneuver up the steep path that led out of the lot and further up the mountain.

As the incline grew more severe, I gripped the back of Gem's light ski jacket. It wasn't just the harder terrain that caused me to hold him—he would never let me fall. What I needed most at that moment was to feel close to him.

I wasn't scoring points with his folks—I knew that. I worried how it would affect us during their visit, but more importantly, what would become of us once they were gone.

I glanced over my shoulder. Where Gem held tight to me, his mother did the same for his father. The grace with which she plowed through the thickening mounds was as natural as the steady leaps of her inner beast. I smiled. For all their sternness as rather stoic personalities, their love was as pure as the surrounding snow.

They didn't return my smile, but yeah, that didn't surprise me. Still, their closeness was something to see. I'd like to think my parents' love would have held strong. But having lost them so young, it wasn't something I would ever know. If nothing else, seeing an elderly couple this devoted was a gift. Claiming and marriage aside, I wanted this with Gemini. But it scared me to want it. Mostly because I knew too many things could take it away.

Love, peeps, didn't guarantee forever.

Gemini leaned into me, reminding me he was still very much there. "I'm going to lift you," he said.

The air thinned with every step I took. I wasn't outdoorsy by any stretch, but I did Zumba, and more recently my share of strip aerobics. I was in good shape. That said, I never shook my ass this high up. "No," I said.

"What?"

He'd practically laughed at me. I couldn't blame him. My breaths were labored and the stomps through the heavy drifts caused my thighs to burn. But I needed to push past it and keep going. "I said no," I insisted.

For once in my life, I didn't mean to be difficult. But seriously, the thought of looking weak just then made me dig my heels in. Gem's parents struck me as people who'd want someone strong at their son's side. It was what he deserved and something I desperately wanted to be for him. "Don't look at me that way, babe. I can't allow you to pick me up."

The corners of his mouth tilted up, and for the first time that day, I saw the adoration that had been lost since his parents' arrival. "And I won't allow my mate to trek through snow this thick and risk harm."

As easily as he spoke, he lifted me into his arms. "Mother's ass," I muttered . . . in time for *his* mother to join us at his side. Her lips pursed tight enough to clutch a lead pipe. Well, of course she'd heard me. Wasn't I just on a roll?

Momma carried Pop in her arms as easily as Gem carried me, only not so cheerfully. Good grief, did these people ever smile? I thought about it. They probably did, just not around me.

Gemini cleared his throat. "Ready?" he asked them.

It should have seemed ridiculous to have such a small elderly woman carry an old man, but somehow, it was right. At least for them, given what they were. If I tried, I might have been able to lift one of Gem's long legs, but not much else.

His mother muttered something in Japanese. At first, I thought it might have been another Taran dig until Gem motioned to the horizon. In the near distance, I saw them: two climbers speeding down the side of a mountain. They were *weres*—they must have been, given the agility and speed with which they descended along the ropes.

Each push off the stone wall caused snow to drift on their heads, and while the high incline appeared long and treacherous, it seemed to tempt the Hamamatsus closer. From where we stood, I could hear the *weres* laughing, drawing more of Momma and Pop's attention. They watched in keen fascination as the *weres* propelled downward and disappeared behind a large mound of snow.

Lex beamed. "You want some of that?" He didn't wait for us to answer. "I can tell that you do—*whoo*! There are three tiers to climb and land on. That there's the longest." He pointed to where the trail grew steeper. "Follow that path—it'll take you to the highest peak, where you can take in the view and start your adventure. One *were*'s positioned at each post, ready when you are—whoo!"

Lex ran ahead of us when we didn't "whoo" back, appearing only slightly deflated, which was more than I could say about me. I looked to Gem's parents, hoping they were willing to go forward.

A small conversation ensued, in Japanese of course. I might have been mistaken, but I thought I heard my name followed by something that sounded like "whore."

I glanced at Gem when they stopped yapping. "Did your mother just call me a whore?" I whispered.

"Ah, no."

"Oh, good."

"But she can hear you."

Her glare told me that yeah, she could.

Awesome.

Gemini grimaced before speaking carefully. "Mother is concerned the climb may be too much for Father but finds the region beautiful and would like to take in the view. Once there, they will consider descending down the wall."

"Oh, that's what I thought she said." I turned to his folks and forced a grin. "Ready to rock and roll?" I asked like a moron.

Their knitted brows told me no, and that I was a skanky liar they'd like to leave here to die. *"Hai,"* they said in the same tone I used on Mancuso.

Gem said something else and crouched. A glimmer of mischief sparkled in Pop's eyes. He said something in a low voice and patted his wife's back. For just a split second, I thought I caught Momma's smile.

Nah. That had to be my imagination. Until Momma took off like a bullet, with Gem speeding toward them. Sweeps of snow drifted along my hair. I huddled closer to him, laughing as he surged forward. "You're going to let her beat you, aren't you?"

Gemini chuckled. "I'm not trying to. My mother was the fastest she-wolf in her village. I doubt she'll give up her title now."

Maybe this was what we needed—some *were* muscle flexing to break the ice. I had a guy carry me once while running on the beach. I didn't weigh much. But even though the guy was fit, he didn't make it far, and it was a jarring run to say the least. With Gem, it was different—smooth and fluid—similar to how I pictured a stream of ink flowing through clear water.

My wolf became one with nature—leaping, pushing faster—his beast embracing the wilderness like he belonged. It was similar to me at a mall. Hey, we all have our strengths.

I blinked back the snowflakes cloaking my eyelashes from the small wisps Momma kicked up. Although their backs were to us, and Pop mumbled in Japanese, I sensed his exhilaration and the encouragement he gave his mate.

"I want that to be us," Gem said quietly. "You and me. I want us to grow old together."

I huddled closer to him, wishing I could promise him forever. But my life had been filled with too many disappointments and more pain than anyone deserved.

He tucked me closer to him. "Do you want that, too?" he

asked. When I didn't answer, he pressed a little further. "Have you given it any thought?"

I was hurting him without even trying, but I couldn't ignore my fears. "Aric told Celia he wanted to grow old with her, just a few weeks back." Despite my prickly tone, I wasn't made of thorns. It hurt me to say what I had to. "At Shayna and Koda's wedding, while they were dancing."

His voice quieted. "I know. He told me."

Although the knowledge shouldn't have made me sadder, it did. "Did he also tell you what else he said—about wanting Celia as his wife, and as the mother to his children?"

"He did."

"He shouldn't have told her," I said. "All it did was hurt her more. Despite what he said, he's still marrying and having children with someone else."

Whatever Gem was feeling gave him an extra boost of speed. He leapt onto a boulder and pushed off another, landing just in front of his parents, never breaking momentum and sprinting ahead. "Aric didn't share those words to hurt her," he said. "He was trying to explain what she means to him because he never told her."

I squeezed my eyes closed tight. I wouldn't cry. *No.* I wouldn't cry. "You're missing the point. Regardless of what he feels, they're no longer together. It would have been better to keep those thoughts to himself."

"Maybe. But Koda and Shayna's wedding triggered feelings he could no longer suppress, especially with Celia so close."

"He should have tried." If I could have, I would have glued my lips shut instead of saying what followed. But maybe Aric wasn't the only one incapable of holding back. "You ask me about forever, when nothing guarantees past today. If your Leader taught me anything, it was that."

10

My words slowed Gem's pace as we reached the mountain's peak, allowing his parents to gain the lead. He skidded to a stop a few paces behind them.

Momma lowered Pop to the ground, barely out of breath. For the first time since I'd met them, they beamed back, until they saw the hurt shadowing our faces.

I forced a smile. For all I'd insisted we enjoy the day, it took all I had not to walk back to our SUV alone. "Your agility is impressive," I said to Momma. "Tomo says you were the fastest *were* in your village."

Her stare bounced to her son before fixing on me. Her nostrils flared discreetly, but I noticed the motion all the same. Instead of simply asking what was wrong, she attempted to use her senses to figure out what happened.

I expected a cruel reprimand, or harsh words. In fact, I steeled myself for it. Instead she nodded. "Shall I tell you about my village over the feast you prepared?"

I didn't move right away. Maybe she was throwing me a

sympathy bone. But in her own way she was trying, despite knowing I had probably hurt her son.

So, I bowed, and reached for the pack. "I'll do it," I said to Gem when he tried to help. His dark brows knitted close. "Please. Let me do this, for you, and your family," I whispered.

For all my insecurities, and despite my defensiveness, I was determined to make this a nice day. Not just for his folks, but because my wolf deserved kindness, too.

I released a breath and pulled the thick flannel blanket just beneath the flap. I'd likely never be able to give my lover everything he wanted, but I could give him this moment between us.

I spread out the blanket with Momma's help. As she took her place beside Pop, she shared her memories of her beloved first home.

"Our village was set in a valley between mountains." She tilted her head. "Not like these, but just as beautiful. Human and *weres* alike worked the rice fields. Wolves like me would race back and forth with baskets filled by hours of hard labor." Her stare grew distant, as if remembering. "We didn't have much, no toys to play with, no pretty dolls, so we made our own games. The one who returned with the most baskets at the end of the day would win a small sack of oranges." Her voice trailed. "To this day, oranges remain among my favorite treat following a meal."

Her voice carried all the warmth of cold lead. But her recollection and the fondness it stirred demonstrated a tenderness I hadn't yet seen. Frigid demeanor or not, this woman did have a heart. I saw it then, and in the way she loved her husband and son.

"I'm sorry," I said. "Had I known oranges were your favorite treat, I would have brought some along." She held out her hand and shook it like it was no biggie, but given how she seemed to cherish the memory, I think it would have meant a great deal to her. "They mean a sweet life, don't they?" I asked.

"Yes." She looked to her husband. "And it has been."

The exchange between them was brief, but so filled with intimacy I turned away as if I were intruding. I rummaged through the pack and yummy, yummy, handed her a bear liver sandwich. She immediately passed it to her husband.

I reached for another to pass to Gemini, but he shook his head. "It's a custom to feed the elders first."

"Oh, okay." I distributed the remaining sandwiches, bottles of water, and potato soup I poured into cups from a thermos.

Pop frowned. "You're not eating liver?" he said.

Again there was my good ol' forced grin. A liver sandwich sounded about as appealing as bread stuffed with bear toes. "I'm good with just soup. Thank you." I lifted my steaming cup. "Bottoms up."

We sat in what I first interpreted as miserable silence until I glanced up and saw the way Momma and Pop took in our surroundings. In my lingering sadness, I hadn't bothered to notice where I sat, and how truly beautiful the scenery was. Those pics on the Net didn't quite capture the ambiance.

This was no mere mountain, nor was it simply a peak swathed in white. This was the Nordic equivalent of Julie Andrews's wet dream. The hills *were* alive. To our left and right, snow-packed peaks reigned over the land, undisturbed by war or industry, time or torment. Despite the harshness of the world, this area had remained as it was, unaffected by the cruelty and pain man had inflicted over time.

For a moment, I simply breathed, wishing I could've been a mountain, or at least shared its strength. Mountains overcame and withstood whatever crossed their paths. Me, I didn't have that superpower. The trauma of my past continued to haunt me. In a way, I'd learned to live with it. I built my walls and muddled through, keeping those dark events from interfering with my life.

Until I met Gemini, and he asked for more than my defenses would allow.

I watched him as he carefully scanned the area. Always aware. Always vigilant. Always kind. God, I wanted him to be happy. But all I managed was to disappoint him.

I meant to inch closer to him, until his parents stood and linked hands, moving toward the edge and disappearing near a patch of woods. *What the . . .?* "Are they going off to have sex?" I whispered.

Gemini closed his eyes and took a breath. "No, Taran."

I tried to peer into the darkness where they'd disappeared. "Are you sure? They were looking kind of cozy."

"Yes. I'm sure." He sighed. "Just like I'm sure they can hear you."

From a short distance away, I heard Momma say something that heated Gem's face.

I groaned. "Sorry, baby."

He didn't answer, staying silent as we gathered our supplies. I removed my glove so I could squeeze his hand with mine and feel the touch of his bare skin. "I don't mean to hurt you," I admitted. "But it's hard for me to believe in forever, when I've seen what love can do and how hard it can hurt when it leaves you."

"It doesn't have to leave you or be as bad as you envision it to be. Look at my parents. They're a prime example of how happy a mated pair can be."

Yet they weren't the norm. I met his face then. "It's hard for me to focus on the beauty of your parents' love when all I can see is my sister's pain."

"Why do you continue to compare us to Aric and Celia? We're different from them."

I forced the truth out even though my mouth told me to shut my trap. "Because Celia has shared the brutality of my life, and because we're more alike than you think."

He leaned back on his heels. "So, because your sister suffers, you will, too?"

I played with the strands of hair that flowed from my hat. "She's taught me a lot. One of those things being how bad it hurts when what you want doesn't work out. I wish I could promise you eternity. But the best I can do is promise right now. Will you let me?"

His dark eyes seemed to see right through me. "For now," was all he'd agree to.

Well, given the choice, it was more than I could ask for.

My phone rang, giving me a good excuse to turn away. I unzipped my thick jacket and pulled it out from the inner pocket. "What's this I hear about you taking on demons at a liquor store? And why did I have to hear it from Misha?"

Celia was hissing though her teeth. That didn't mean Gemini didn't hear every word. His head whipped my way and he snarled. I pinched the bridge of my nose. Sweet merciful heavens, I so didn't need this. "Not now, okay, Ceel?"

"Not now? Are you kidding me!"

"Ceel, I'm with Gem's family," I snapped.

"I know," she shot back. "But this is important."

Can't be that important if her vamp waited a whole day to tell her. "I said, *not now*."

"Taran, you don't understand," she said. "The vamps discovered something in the rear of the shop—something that shouldn't have been there."

I shuddered, thinking back to that little naked creature and his set of nasty tongues. While I didn't want to know what the vamps uncovered, I didn't have a choice, did I? "More demons?" I guessed.

"No, *cages*, Taran. The store owner had been keeping them . . . and feeding them. The vamps found four empty cages and leftover human parts."

It was a good thing I'd finished my soup because I didn't

think I'd be eating anytime soon. Gem caught my phone when it slipped from my grasp. "Celia, it's Gemini. Where is the owner now?"

"Gone," she said.

Gemini frowned. "He escaped the vampires?"

"No, Gem," she answered. "He's dead . . ."

11

---

ow could you keep a demon attack from me?"

"**H**   For all that Gem was trying to be quiet, he wasn't succeeding. "Believe it or not, I did it for you," I muttered under my breath.

"For me? How does this benefit me, or anyone—and how is it that your first call is to the leeches?"

I glanced over at his parents. Lex was helping Pop with his helmet and his partner was securing Momma to the harness. Oh, and look, they were pissed, too. "Can we discuss this later? I'm trying to make this a nice day for you, damnit!"

"No. We will discuss it now."

I tossed the rope I was instructed to wind onto the hard-packed snow. "Fine. It happened at the state store when I was picking up your father's sake. I didn't know the owner was housing them—feeding them—whatever the he was doing with them. I just wanted the fucking sake!" I threw out a hand at the sound of Gem's parents' audible gasps. "Sorry, I meant—oh forget it," I mumbled.

It was too late; everyone was angry even before I "fucked" the sake. "Gem. He didn't give me any indication he was a Tribe *were.* It was a liquor store—not some crazy prison camp stuffed with innocent people."

"It was a *front,*" Gem said. His scowl matched his parents'. In fact, the resemblance was uncanny. "A temporary place to house demons they were transporting."

"Well, yeah. I get it now."

Gemini snarled for all he was worth. "If you would have called me, there wouldn't have been anything to 'get' now. I would have determined something was wrong upon my arrival. Did you even stop to consider why there were demons there?"

"Of course, I did. I'm not stupid. But I needed to get back to *you.*"

For a moment he simply froze. "*You're* angry at *me?*"

"Of course, I'm angry. You're yelling at me."

"And why do you think I'm yelling? Taran, if you had called me, Aric, Koda, Liam—any *were* you know—we might have been able to track down their location. But you didn't. You—"

"I called the 'leeches.' Yeah, yeah, I know. You don't like them, or trust them, and are convinced they're out for prom queens and their own gain, and you're probably right." I shoved my hands on my hips. "But you forget, you were picking up your folks. I couldn't call Aric, or Koda, and especially Liam, because they would have run and told you. I didn't want you dropping everything to rush to a situation I was handling. So, I called the Alliance members who would help, who would keep it quiet and buy me the time I needed to do something nice for your parents."

Gem didn't budge. "I should have been your first call," he repeated.

"Maybe. And I'm sorry. But I can't go back to make this right."

I lifted the rope and edged to the cliff to look out, mostly because I couldn't stand the hurt shadowing my lover's face.

Vamps had excellent noses and could track to some extent. But they didn't possess the hunting skills of a *were*.

Gem was right, I should have called Aric. Yet as stupid as it sounds, I would have felt like I was betraying Celia.

I meant well. But Gem couldn't see past my call to the vamps, which sucked. I reached for the spare helmet close to my feet. Not the cutest thing I'd ever wear, but I needed to keep going. No matter how bad I wanted to curl into a warm bed and forget this horrible afternoon.

Pop strode to my side. I almost smiled. He looked so cute in his safety harness and climbing gear. But his irate scowl made it clear he wasn't happy with me, either. "Tribe *weres* are keeping demons in the area."

He wasn't asking, he was informing me that he'd heard our chat.

I kicked at the snow at my feet. "Yes. The store owner who sold me your sake and I were attacked yesterday—the day you arrived. He didn't give me any indication he was a Tribesman; in fact, he was scared stupid when he saw them." I shrugged. "But given how they ate his face and all, I can't really blame him."

"What did he say about the dark ones?"

"Nothing. According to my sister, he exploded to bits when the vamps questioned him."

Pop frowned. "When a stray *were* or outcast vamp is inducted into the Tribe, a spell is placed on him to keep their secrets and keep them committed. If they talk, they explode," I explained. "The vamps must have been very convincing. Too bad he detonated before they were able to get much out of him."

"I'm aware of the spell and what it does," Pop said.

He wasn't demeaning despite his even tone. It was more like he was making me aware of how much he knew about the supernaturals and the war. So then why was he frowning? "I apologize if I'm coming across as rude. But if you're familiar with the silencing spell, why are you looking at me like that? Is something bothering you?" *And if it is, please don't let it be me.*

"Aiko is committed as a *were* to defend and protect the earth," he began. "As my mate, I join and support her cause. I don't understand those who seek harm. It's something I've never understood."

Yeah, well, same here, Pop. I glanced behind me to where Gemini stood with his back to me. He spoke low and quickly into his phone—probably to Aric—spilling the details the "leeches" had uncovered. His voice was gruff and angry, and his stance rigid, as if preparing to lunge. So not what I wanted to hear or see.

God, what a screw-up I was.

I turned back to Pop. This man would never be all butterflies and rainbows, but at least he was speaking to me and standing by me.

He crossed his arms, staring out into the horizon. "The owner probably didn't know what he was getting into," he said. "Demon children are hard to maintain and control. Their desire for human meat makes them little more than crazed predators. No conscience. No respect for life. Only the need to feed." He looked at me then. "Tell me what the vampires discovered."

I lifted the rope from the ground and untangled the knots. "Celia—my sister—said the locks were still secure around the cages. My guess is they somehow slipped through the bars."

"Hai," Pop agreed. "They've been known to break their rib cages to squeeze through small spaces. The owner must not have fed them well enough. If he had, they wouldn't have been so desperate to escape and hunt."

He was right. "A local pack on the Nevada side found the fresh remains of tourists," I told him. "The bite marks suggest they were used as demon kibble. But from what I know, there haven't been more bodies discovered, so I'm wondering if the Tribe just ran out of food for them." At least, that's what I hoped. Problem was, less food meant more hungry and desperate predators on the loose.

Pop's stern face tightened more than I thought was humanly possible. "What of the other cages?" he asked.

"What?"

"You said there were four cages, but only two demon children present—the ones you killed, correct?"

I involuntarily shuddered. "Celia says the other two cages had been used at some point, but the scents within them were older."

"How old?" Pop asked.

I grimaced. "A few days, maybe longer. Looks like there are more out there."

"Hai," he said again. "The Tribesmen are trying to maintain the numbers they have following all the Alliance raids."

"That's what Aric says," I mumbled.

Pop nodded. "He's a good, smart Leader," he said.

Not when it came to my sister, I obviously didn't say back.

Something flickered in Pop's face. "What is it?" I asked him.

"Tribesmen are feeding demons they can't control."

I huffed. "Yeah. Tell me about it."

His stern face met mine. "Which means something else is controlling them."

I hadn't thought about it. Mostly because I hadn't wanted to. "A Tribesmaster?" I offered, although I didn't want it to be true. Unlike demons—the ones straight from hell—Tribemasters were spawn of a demon and a powerful witch. Demon children were spawn of demons or Tribemasters and a non-magical human. Any combo was totally hideous, but the Tribemasters were a different breed of scary. Unlike demons, they had an unlimited time on earth, and unlike their mindless demon children spawn, they had cunning—making them cruel, lethal, and shrewd.

"Let's hope it's only a mature demon child," I added.

You know your life is a nightmare when this was the better option of the two.

"Let's hope," Pop agreed.

Momma strode over, her lovely scowl firmly in place. In a strange way, I'd become used to it, mostly because it was all I knew. Lex bounded right behind her. He smacked his hands together and rubbed them hard. "You folks ready for a climb of a lifetime—*whoo*!"

Christ above, again with the "whoos." My eyes danced to Gem. He disconnected his call and pocketed the phone in his jacket before taking a large step back. I thought it was odd but didn't think too much of it and returned to his folks.

Lex clipped the rope onto Momma's safety harness. "On belay," he said, acknowledging the clip was in place.

"Belay on," Momma answered like a seasoned pro. Her rigid expression made her appear bored and possibly constipated.

Pop mirrored her features. "Aiko is very excited," he said.

"It shows," I lied.

Lex adjusted the rope around his waist connecting him and Momma, while his partner disappeared down the path and to the next steep as instructed. "This here is the highest point," Lex said. "Now, ma'am, I'm here to be your safety. Take your time, take in the view, and jet down at your own pace. No need to worry, just enjoy it. *Whoo*!"

Pop edged as close to the ledge as he could and whispered something in Japanese. I wasn't the cute and cuddly type, but I found them endearing in their own way. "Climb," Lex said.

Although Lex was probably a pro, his "whoo-whoos" made me nervous, and my encounter with the store owner more than a little paranoid. I lifted the extra coil of rope at his feet and snaked it around my arms.

He turned and winked. "Don't you trust me, sugarplum?"

"I'm not your sugarplum. And if you drop her, I'll roast your balls like kabobs." I grinned and waved to Momma and Pop. "It's okay, I've got her!"

Their slackened jaws remained their only response . . . and my cue they'd heard my interaction with Lex the stoner. With one last exchange, Momma began her descent. I tossed a glance over my shoulder; somewhat surprised Gem hadn't growled when Lex called me "sugarplum." And maybe somewhat disappointed, too.

He simply stood there, watching the spot before him until something caused his spine to straighten. The air stirred and the aroma of dry herbs trickled into my nose, making me sneeze. In a swirl of deep gold and bright yellow tendrils, Genevieve appeared, spinning in place and stopping directly in front of my wolf.

Their eyes met. Gem spoke low, quickly. Vieve listened intently, as if no one else existed, as if nothing else mattered, and as if his *girlfriend* wasn't standing a few yards away. She nodded, clinging to every muttering—every syllable—every *breath*!

I didn't think they could get any closer. But when it was her turn to speak, Gem leaned forward so she could whisper in his ear, her perfect lips close to his skin.

Maybe it was the day.

Or our fight.

Or this whole experience.

Or maybe Genevieve was just a man-stealing slut.

Something in me flared. A wave of anger I'd never known. He wouldn't talk to me—in fact, he'd *yelled.* But to Genevieve, it was all soft words and attention he hadn't bothered to show me since the arrival of his parents.

Gemini lowered his eyelids, taking in everything that

wicked witch had to say, so close, so intimate—almost touching, almost *kissing.*

Rage burned inside me, igniting my magic and shooting bolts of lightning up and over my head. Gem's head whipped in my direction; his eyes wide as my power released in a jaw-rattling surge from my hands. *"Taran!"*

He barreled toward me. But his focus was further ahead. I reeled around in time to see a current of blue and white light snake along the rope, electrifying Lex and launching him into the stand of pines with a yelp.

Holy heavens! Momma's anchor was gone.

Gem plowed ahead, soaring into the air, reaching for the end of the rope, and . . . missed. To my horror, I watched the sizzling rope disappear over the cliff.

With a grunt and what—Jesus *Christ*—sounded like a *splat,* Momma Hamamatsu landed on the steep below.

"Oh shit. Oh, hell. Oh *fuck!*" I bolted forward, sprawling onto my belly between Gem and his father.

Way, *way* down below, Momma lay spread-eagle, her charred boots smoldering several feet away from her, having freaking *exploded* from her feet. The remains of the rope twitched and sputtered blue and white light around her unmoving form. If it weren't for the glare fixed on her face, I would have sworn she was dead.

She sat up, causing her shattered helmet to fall away in pieces and revealing the outline of her body singed into the slab of rock beneath her. Smoke, I kid you not, wafted from her fricasseed hair. I wanted to die. I seriously wanted to die.

Gemini and Pop called to her, speaking rapidly in Japanese.

Funny enough, her attention was all on me.

12

My sisters spread out along my king-sized bed. They blinked back at me as I took another sip of wine, and another one after that. Celia opened her mouth, then closed it, before holding out her hand. "I'm sorry—I'm sorry," she said. "Let me see if I got this straight. You *threw* Gemini's *mother* off the side of a cliff?"

I took another sip and leaned back against my headboard. "Yup."

"A *cliff,*" Celia repeated.

"A big one," I answered, my voice oddly numb.

Emme clutched one of the pillows and pressed it against her. "That's . . .awful."

"Ya think?" I snapped.

"But she was all right, right?" Shayna's stare bounced around the room like she wasn't sure where to look, disbelief spreading like fire around her features. "I mean she's *were,* so she should recover, right?"

"Yes," I answered stiffly. "But that's not exactly the point, is it?" I placed the wine on the side table and dug my fingers through my hair. "It could have been Pop, or I could have killed her. How do you apologize for something like that?"

"You can start by saying sorry," Emme offered.

"I did—don't you think I did?" I dropped my hands away. "This has been a nightmare. I've tried, really I have. But nothing's worked out. They've seen my nipple, for crying out loud!"

Emme grimaced. "Ah, yeah, that was unfortunate."

"Unfortunate? It was one step shy of porn." I stood and started pacing. "There's no way to fix this. No way to look good. Is there?"

"No. Nope. No way, dude," they all muttered at once.

I was sort of counting on their optimism, but the fact that these three couldn't find one silver lining in the monumental crap storm this experience had become demonstrated just how bad things sucked.

Celia stood, tugging her stretchy shirt down over her skinny jeans. "What does Gemini say about everything?"

"He hasn't said anything. The whole drive back to the lodge where his parents are staying, didn't say a word. No one did. He mumbled something about returning later when he dropped me off, but he hasn't called or texted since."

Shayna cocked her head. "So where is he, then, T?" she asked, fiddling with the ends of her long, dark ponytail.

And there was the snap, crackle, and pop of my magic again. "He's with Genevieve. Where else would he be, Shayna?"

Celia leaned back on her heels. "I see," she said.

Shayna puckered a brow. "I don't," she admitted. "She's head wand-waver, dude. I'm sure the furries and the Hermione Granger sorority girls are just working together to figure out where these demon smugglers are headed."

Celia shook her head. "Shayna, it's not that I don't agree—I know Gemini is only strategizing."

"Then what's wrong, Celia?" Emme asked quietly, her soft green eyes carrying all the sadness I felt.

Celia bowed her head. "It's how their interaction is making her feel."

I wished I could deny it, but I couldn't. My girl, Celia, nailed exactly what I was feeling. I walked to where I'd left my wine-glass and reached for it, but then changed my mind. "I think I have to break up him. End things now while I can still salvage what remains of me."

"Wait—*what*?" Celia's attention shot my way. "Taran, that's not why I'm suggesting at all."

Emme could barely speak. "T-Taran, how could you even contemplate something so extreme?"

"Yeah, T," Shayna said. "I mean you're, like, *mates*."

"Please don't use that word in front of me," I stammered. A lump claimed my throat as I shook my head. "I'm clearly not meant for this."

"*Matehood?*" Shayna lifted her hands in surrender. "I'm only asking, T."

"No, *happiness*," I managed, a sinking feeling filling my chest.

I adjusted the ties to my silk robe, unable to take the stunned silence my sisters met me with. "I stumbled into this relationship, and kidnappings, demon invasions, and infected vampires aside, it's been amazing. But I've kept it at arm's length, knowing this would happen."

"Knowing what would happen, exactly?" Celia's voice was quiet, concerned, and while I could feel Shayna and Emme waiting for me to respond, I kept my attention on her.

"That it wouldn't end well, Ceel. I don't think happiness is something I'm meant to have. Look at what we've been through, and what we've survived. Every time something good happens, it's like something bad must happen, too. It's like some kind of twisted scale balancing the good and the bad. Gem's been the good. But this whole meet-the-parents thing—it's been bad. Really bad. And I can't help thinking it's a glimpse of what's to come."

Celia stepped forward. "Taran, I know this hasn't been the best experience for you."

"Celia, that's putting it lightly, and I'm not just talking about his folks here. Look at us—look at our lives. We have these powers"— I held out my hands and engulfed my fingers with fire —"as a result of a curse meant to kill us. This curse may have backfired and given us magic, but it also took our parents in exchange. I'm starting to think we're cursed in a lot more ways than one."

Shayna shook her head. "I think you're overreacting."

"Am I?" I shake out my hands, putting out the flames. "Look at everything we've been through. Don't you think it's odd how much we've suffered for how young we are?"

Shayna smiled through her forming tears. "But I have Koda. And I'm happy."

"And I hope you always will be, Shayna," I said, truthfully. "But I'm not sure Gemini and I will be as lucky. . . I don't think we're going to make it."

The door opened then, and Gemini stepped inside, his expression as warm as those of his beloved parents. He hadn't bothered knocking, but for the time being this was his room, too. The thing was, I knew him well enough to know he'd heard me. And maybe my sisters did, too.

Emme and Shayna slipped off the bed. "Hi, Gem," they both mumbled quietly as they passed.

Gemini tilted his head in acknowledgment, but he squared his sights on me. He wasn't happy. *Well, join the club.*

Celia was the only one who didn't scamper away. "Did you find anything?" she asked. Unlike my other sisters, she didn't bother with a polite hello. I couldn't blame her. She knew things were just that bad.

Gem cast his gaze in her direction. "The coven was able to

conduct a tracking spell at the store. It wasn't strong enough to see in which direction the demons had been transported in or out, but it was strong enough to detect other fronts in the area."

"Well, yippee for witches," I muttered. "All their wand-waving is finally paying off for them."

Gemini stiffened at the slight but continued. "We were able to organize a few raids, incarcerate several Tribesmen, and destroy about a dozen demon children. But every time the pack's come close to obtaining information, we lose the Tribe *were* or vamp in question to the silencing spell placed upon them."

Celia pushed back her thick, wavy hair. "Any idea why they chose this area? It doesn't make sense to bring demons this close to the lake. They wouldn't survive long."

Gem rubbed his goatee. "Our best guess is that there was another stronghold close to here, but our constant presence and aggressive patrols are forcing the Tribe to move out of the region."

"With a nursery of demon children in tow," Celia offered.

Gem nodded. "The impact we've had on the war has made our enemies desperate. They're trying to cling to what they have, and what they have are demon children. But as effective as demons are as weapons, they need to be fed, transported to safety, and given time to grow."

I rubbed my temples. "Problem is, it doesn't take long for these suckers to grow. And when they do, the Tribe is going to unleash them in droves."

Gem, although he didn't disagree, kept his stiff tone. "Their growth may be quick, but their temperament has worked to our advantage. Transferring creatures so volatile and strong can't be accomplished in large numbers without risk of discovery. So, they've been brought in in small groups, cared for, and moved out."

"So South Tahoe is nothing more than a half-way point to

wherever they're headed?" Celia asked.

"That's what we've determined," Gem answered. "But which direction they're going remains unclear. From what we've uncovered, everything points to the east—toward the Nevada side. The west side is too close to the Den and discovery."

"That still leaves a huge area to cover." I sighed when he turned my way. "Just because I'm upset doesn't mean I'm not listening."

"I never claimed you weren't listening," he countered.

Yup. And that was Ceel's cue to leave. She glanced from me to Gem, worry creasing her beautiful face. "I should go," she said. "If you need backup, don't hesitate to call." She walked slowly toward the door, pausing when her hand touched the doorknob. "We'll talk later. Okay, Taran?"

"Looking forward to it." I slumped on the side of my bed when Gem simply stared, his features alternating between anger, frustration, and worry, but mostly disappointment. I'd disappointed him, *again.* I hurt him, *again.* How could things be so ass-suckingly miserable?

I buried my face in my hands, trying not scream, but mostly trying not to cry for us. Was it over? That's what it felt like then. I'd tried so hard. I really had.

Gemini reached for my hands, taking each one carefully. I raised my chin to find him kneeling before me, my jaw clenching so tight it pained my gums. God, I was angry, and hurt, and, *humiliated.* He'd left me for Genevieve when I'd needed him most. Okay, not really. Protecting the earth came first; I got it. But it was hard knowing he was with her when I'd needed him with me.

"Hi," he said. When I didn't answer, his gaze softened. "You feel far away from me. My wolves and I hate it—*we* hate it. I don't want us to fight. Will you let me hold you?"

It was then that I threw my arms around him like a wimp.

"You left me," I said.

"No." He gathered me to him, stroking my hair. "I stepped in to execute the duties as second in command. Nothing more."

"That's not what it felt like." My throat twisted into a painful knot. "Especially given who you left me for."

"I would never leave you for another." His body curled around mine. "You're the only one I see and desire."

I clutched him tighter, wishing I could hold him forever as my insecurities spilled from my mouth. "I went into this whole thing with you and your folks kicking and screaming. But despite my mistakes I committed to it. I did my best to make them like me, and I failed at every turn." My voice trembled. "You might have noticed today wasn't our best day."

He stilled with his palm between my shoulder blades. "The introduction of my parents has . . . not gone as I'd hoped."

"No shit," I muttered. I pulled away and trailed my fingers down the side of his face. "How's your mother?"

"She's well," he answered.

His silence told me what I already knew. "She hates me . . . They both do, don't they?" Who was I kidding? *Hate* was probably not a strong enough word.

"It's not that they hate you, Taran," he finally said. "It's simply that . . . they haven't seen . . ." He worked his jaw. "They just don't know you," he added quickly.

My hands slipped away from his neck. "Really? This is the best you can do?" I stood and walked to the window looking out to the front of the house, although I couldn't see anything past the disaster this day had been.

"Tonight is another moment for grace and understanding," he said. "Let's get dressed, go to dinner as planned, and try again."

"I can't go, babe," I told him truthfully. I pressed my hands against the window ledge and leaned forward. "You go with them. You won't screw things up. If I show, locusts will swarm the building and a plague will unleash upon the earth before we even get our salads."

Strong, reassuring arms circled my waist. "This is my parents' last night. I need you with me, as my mate, and my love . . ."

I choked down the sob his words stirred.

"Our time with them has not been ideal," he continued. "But every intention came from your heart." He kissed my head. "And that's all I can ask."

"But they *hate* me," I insisted.

He didn't exactly deny it. "Taran, regardless of what my parents think or feel, I love you. No one could ever change what you mean to me."

I wasn't so sure. I turned around and crossed my arms. Whatever emotion Gem saw in my features caused him to frown and hardened his stance. He stepped forward, his strong body pressing against me, his gaze claiming mine. My eyes widened briefly, only for my lids to lower and my heart to thump. As I watched, his hand fumbled to close the blinds.

I knew what he wanted before he touched me, before his fingers peeled off my robe and panties in quick, fluid motions, and long before he lifted my hips and hooked my ankles behind his back.

I knew because I wanted it, too. We both needed to feel something other than uncertainty. We needed that something good only our bodies could give us.

At first his kisses and wandering hands were slow and reassuring, his way of proving he was here with me, and not going anywhere. But I wanted more—his passion, his lust, and maybe his aggression to prove how hard he could love me. So, when his hands smoothed across my bare skin, my teeth found the curve of his neck, and my nails his firm ass.

A guttural moan broke through his throat, my aggression

inciting my lover to tap into the beasts caged inside him and fuel the man holding me in his grip.

Good. I didn't want slow, or gentle, or careful. I wanted primal hunger, a man barely in control. Just as I wanted the stiffness sliding across my belly and prodding me hard.

My breath hitched with how fast he pinned me against the wall, his urgency to enter me sending chills along my limbs. My body, although ready to accept his, wasn't enough. Not for someone my lover's size. I gritted my teeth as he rubbed against me, his smooth skin stroking me and stimulating those tightening regions that begged for his touch.

Slowly, he made his way in, both of us cursing when he filled me. I clasped his jaw, my eyelids heavy and my irises swimming with lust. He growled at my inviting smile just once before crashing his lips against mine.

It had taken him time to enter, but that leisurely pace was now long forgotten. He withdrew, only to slam into me hard. Again. Again. And again, forcing my body to slide against the cool wall.

"More," I begged. "Please more."

And that's exactly what he gave me.

This position minimized my movements and allowed him to seize all control. I wasn't subservient by any stretch, but I made exceptions when it came to Gem and our moments alone. So instead of dominating, I allowed myself to succumb, welcoming every inch of him, the aggression behind those thrusts, and his strong body pressed against me.

My legs flailed uselessly and sweat poured down my back in rivers as his hips rammed me. I screamed his name, pleaded for him to go faster, and spoke dirty words to fuel our passion.

I bucked—trying to move, trying to breathe, trying to do more than scream with pleasure. God, what was he doing to me?

Whatever he did, I could only plead for more, refusing mercy and urging him forward with the tilts of my pelvis.

My heart threatened to punch through my chest. Sex with Gemini was going to kill me. I knew it then. A sinful smile spread across my face. Yeah, and what a way to go. I bounced against the wall with every grind of his hips, every deep thrust, begging him not to stop, to go harder until I surrendered to the wave of pleasure engulfing me.

My nails dug into his shoulders when I lost control, my way of trying to endure the ardor tightening my core. As the wave peaked and my legs kicked out, I squeezed my eyes tight. Tears of pleasure streamed along my cheeks, but my lover wasn't done with me yet. Another wave of ecstasy struck before the first could fully cease.

I didn't feel him move us, too blinded by one last mind-blowing orgasm that bowed my spine. My back hit the mattress with Gem falling on top of me, panting hard, while I struggled to take large gulps of the sex-charged air.

My eyes met his, my body quivering from the rush, and the way he took me in. "I love you," he gasped. "Nothing will ever change who you are to me."

13

___

I had this great idea—a seriously kick-ass idea. The Grizzly's Song was one of the premier restaurants in the world, renowned for its breathtaking views and exotic dishes that ranged from venison to pheasant. Meals comprised of game meat, peeps. *Game.* Wolves like that sort of crap, right? So, I called in another favor to Misha once I discovered the waiting list was three months long and booked us a table for four.

Well, we all know how well my great ideas had gone during this little meet-and-greet adventure. Because of the restaurant's remoteness, the path leading up the mountain was, let's just say, from *hell.* I don't think we passed more than two cars along the way. Mostly, I think local residents were smarter than we were and knew to avoid what was apparently nature's version of the spin cycle. I don't get carsick, ever. I did then.

Momma and Pop? Their heads hung out the windows long before we pulled into the restaurant's circular drive. The valet opened the SUV door, a big smile firmly in place. "Good evening. I'm Kevin. Welcome to the Grizzly's Song. How is your evening?"

"My evening sucks, Kevin!" I slipped around him and threw open the rear passenger-side door. Momma's lovely pursed lips and snow-white face greeted mine. I whirled on Kevin. "What kind of sadist designed your roads? Look at her. She's nothing short of death on French toast—no offense, Momma."

Kevin must have heard this rant several times in his valet parking career and kept his grin. "Oh, yes, the road to the Grizzly is quite windy. Which is why we offer a helicopter service at the bottom of the mountain for an additional fee."

Okay, wasn't aware of that one. Thanks, Kevin, for making me look like a cheap bastard. I turned back to Momma and tried to help her out of the SUV. She glared at my hand but allowed me to assist her. Yeah, *Steel Magnolias* is bullshit. This woman would never give me a kidney.

Her skin returned to its normal olive tone when we reached the top of the stacked stone steps. But she had a wolf to restore her and ease her nausea. Pop didn't. He only had his son, who practically carried him out of the rear. We should have turned around twenty minutes ago, but Siri insisted we were almost there. Well, we would have been if the road were a straight line rather than a hideous spiral that made our bellies churn.

Pop draped his arm around Gemini and leaned heavily against him. "Maybe the fresh mountain air will help?" I offered rather desperately.

Pop responded by puking all over the second step. Some guy appeared with a hose. I guessed it wasn't the first time some poor sap spilled his stomach contents here at the Grizzly. Momma hurried to her husband, but not before one less-than-enthusiastic glimpse my way.

If it were possible to nut-punch the "Grizzly" I would have then.

Lᴇᴛ's just say dinner wasn't fun. Every time Gem or I tried to initiate conversation, his parents remained tight-lipped. In all fairness, Pop wasn't feeling well, and Momma was clearly worried about him and likely pissed at me. Gemini, in his last-ditch effort to make me look good, made a show of explaining how famous the restaurant was, the exotic cuisine that changed with each season, and how it was all my genius plan.

Yay for me.

As it was, my stomach remained topsy-turvy following the windy ride. I took a few sips of my quail soup and some bites of bread, which is more than poor Pop managed. Gemini and his mother didn't feel right eating without him and requested their meals be wrapped.

Forty-three minutes. That was how long we lasted at the Grizzly, including the time it took us to pay the tab. Pathetically enough, it was only two whole minutes more than the drive there.

Gem slipped into the SUV after tipping the valet, who continued to grin as if my world wasn't imploding around me. I glanced toward the backseat, where Pop lay slumped across Momma's lap. If she wasn't with him, I'd be flinging myself over the seats and starting chest compressions, thoroughly convinced the old guy had coded.

I quickly turned around when my stomach twisted as Gem took the first bend. "Are you all right?" he asked me.

I tried to shake my head, but that only made me dizzy and churned the quail soup fighting to stay down. "I'm sorry," I said, meaning it, but Jesus, how many times could I apologize?

"It's not your fault," he said quietly. "You meant well."

I sighed. Yeah, and how many more times could he say that? Gem's dark eyes were marked with worry as he maneuvered the vehicle around the perilous turns. I didn't like it one bit. While he'd never expressed what he'd hoped to accomplish from my encounter with his parents, it was obvious nothing had gone as planned. "I'm sorry," I said again, since maybe I couldn't say it enough.

"Taran . . ." was all he managed.

He slowed the SUV as we rounded a more precarious curve. The rest of us collectively groaned. Good God, we weren't even halfway down the mountain yet.

I lowered my window to breathe in some air, only for screams to punch through the opening. Gemini screeched the SUV to a stop in time to see a group of men dragging a man and a woman from their vehicle.

My magic stirred a warning as Momma yelled, "Vampires, Tomo!"

She was right. And their protruding fangs and bloodthirsty eyes told me they planned to do more than feed.

Gemini flung open the door. "Stay here!" he yelled.

Yeah, right.

I hit the seatbelt release and bounded out, stomping as fast as my platform heels could take me. The cold mountain air struck my face, slapping the nausea down and forcing me to take in the scene ahead of me. As he ran, Gemini shrugged out of his jacket and tossed it aside. From one leap to the next, his twin wolf ripped through his dress shirt, cutting in front of him and tackling the closest vamp. One wolf joined the other as Gem's remaining half *changed*.

Bloody ash spilled from his powerful fangs as he fought the other vampires. But I couldn't stop and watch. I stumbled to where the woman lay motionless on the ground. I shrugged her shoulder, shaking her hard. "Hey, are you okay?"

I recognized too late she was also a vampire. Sharp nails dug into my throat as she hoisted me from the ground. But I wasn't helpless, and she was messing with the wrong chick. With a pained grunt, my fire of blue and white engulfed me, igniting her in a wash of flame.

Ash exploded in my face as my body struck the ground. I

rolled onto my side, grunting from the impact. "Gem, it's a trap!"

I'd barely choked the words out when another SUV screeched around the bend and more hissing vampires charged out. From behind me, another loud engine roared.

An old utility truck sped forward to where Momma was lifting Pop's slumped form from our vehicle. The truck was gunning for them, ready to mow them down. I raced forward, unleashing my power in one primal scream.

Blue and white electrified heat rocketed from my core, spiraling and striking the truck's face. The impact born of rage and fire flipped the truck directly above Momma, who curled against her mate's limp form. In a burst of angry flames, the truck soared over the guardrail, the impact of the crash shaking the mountain.

A whooshing sound and a pained snarl had me reeling back to the other fight. Tribesmen in the forms of two wolves bounded toward me. I crouched low, my hands shaking with the energy crackling in my palms. "Come on, Mommy's waiting for you," I said under my breath.

I rammed my hands out, the bolts I released spinning like blades and slicing the wolves in half. My head whipped around, searching for Gem, only to catch sight of the vamps closing in on Momma and Pop.

Momma carefully released Pop and stood slowly, her body unmoving while her eyes took in the encroaching vamps. I ran forward, cursing, knowing I wouldn't reach them in time before the first vamp attacked.

I wasn't fast, but my power was.

I fell forward and slapped my hands against the asphalt. My magic released the moment my palms connected with the road, sending a ripple of fire in a building crest of blue and white light. The ripple swelled, striking the hissing vampires' backs and engulfing them in fire.

Momma lifted Pop over her shoulder, bounding over the flames and away from the fight. They were safe, but not for long. The sound of peeling tires alerted me that more Tribesmen had arrived. I couldn't see them over the billowing smoke overtaking our surroundings, but I knew they were there, and that the danger was far from over.

I looked right and left, trying to get a sense of what would attack next. The energy I expended rivaled that of my biggest supernatural brawls. But I wasn't done, and I refused to let Pop and Momma perish.

A werecat punched through the smoke. I released my lightning, singeing its snout off, but missed the werecougar charging behind him.

I lashed out again, detonating its skull with my lightning and killing it mere feet from where I stood. Yet as hard as we fought, we were outnumbered and trapped. But it was what happened next that robbed my lungs of air. Gem's black wolf, the one with a white left paw, rocked from side to side, abandoning his prey before collapsing onto the road.

My hands trembled with energy as I released more lightning and raced toward him. But my efforts were in vain. A gun blast followed an odd *whooshing* sound. A sharp, stinging pain pierced my back. I remember trying to scream before the vampire jetting toward me morphed into a blur of color and everything faded into darkness.

14

I blinked my heavy eyelids open as glimpses of the attack fought their way through the fog continuing to dull my senses. I tried to swallow, coughing from the dryness stretching from my throat to my belly.

At first, I thought the fight had been nothing more than a bad and twisted dream, since all I initially felt was Gem's naked body on top of mine. But this wasn't our bed, and Toto, we were a long-ass way from Kansas.

We lay huddled in a corner. Cold, dank air claimed the parts of my body his large form failed to shield. I shuddered. But it wasn't just because of the chill. It was because our night had gone from bad to dangerous, then landed headfirst into deadly.

Dim light from a small bulb shone through heavy metal bars a few feet away, cutting lines into the concrete floor. The Tribesmen had apparently shoved us into a large cell. Wall-to- wall cinder block pressed against our backs like cold and lecherous hands. I tried to push the strands of hair gathered around my face only to discover my hands were bound behind me. *"God,"* I muttered.

Gem stilled above me. "You're awake," he said, sounding relieved.

"Awake and pissed." I struggled against the handcuffs, but all I did was dig the metal into my skin. When I tried to kick my legs out, it occurred to me that hey, look at that, they were shackled, too. "Where are we?"

He released a growl intermixed with a frustrated breath. "The Tribe stronghold where they've been housing the demon children."

"You *have* to be kidding me."

The nearby flapping of wings followed by rather enthusiastic and wet munching confirmed his suspicions. Awesome. Just awesome.

Fear pumped adrenaline through me, shaking off whatever tranquilizer the vamps had shot me with. Everywhere I looked, I caught sight of something new and more gruesome. Deep claw marks scarred the concrete floor, the bars in front of us, and the cinder-block wall. Whatever had been caged before us had fought to escape. The stained red concrete made it clear it hadn't made it out in one piece, if it had made it at all.

"Are you hurt, Taran?" Gem asked.

It was then that I realized how hoarse he sounded. My head pounded from stress and my throat throbbed where the vamp had choked me. But I was alive.

At least for now.

"Some bruising, but nothing serious . . ." My voice trailed as I realized who was missing. "Gem, where are your parents?"

"In the cell beside ours."

"Are they okay?"

"Father is weak from vomiting, but Mother is well and keeping him warm."

"And, how are you?" He sounded awful. As he edged off me I tried to sit up, waiting for him to tell me he was fine.

But he wasn't.

A gold spear extending past his shoulders circled tight against his throat, and gold shackles bound his wrists and ankles. Sweat poured down his face. I wasn't sure how long we'd been out, but it didn't take long for cursed gold to sicken a *were* or vamp.

I tried to scoot closer. "Jesus, baby . . . are you okay?"

His face momentarily flushed only for beads of sweat to form along his forehead. "The gold from the shackles is taking its toll, and there's a bullet lodged in my stomach. My twin is too weak to leave me with all the gold encasing us."

My eyes swept over his paling skin. Blood caked his abdominal muscles, but I didn't see a wound. "It healed," he said before I could ask.

I crinkled my brow. "Then it's not gold, right? If it was, it would burn and keep the wound open, correct?"

"Yes. But something isn't right. I'm not sure what it is, but there's something odd about the alloy. I don't know if it's tainted with magic or cursed, but its negative effects are poisoning my body." His hard expression met mine. "We have to get out of here."

Slurp, slurp, chomp, chomp, followed by more excited flapping. I pushed aside the chills those freak demons riled and tried to think. "Can you *change*?"

His hoarse voice stiffened. "No, this device around my neck is jagged. If I *change,* it will slice my head off."

I swore under my breath. "They were looking for food, weren't they? And I take it we're their groceries?"

"For their leeches and demons," he answered. My blood boiled over, this time with fear I could no longer suppress. I nuzzled up against him for comfort as he continued. "From what I heard, they're to move out by nightfall." He waited as if debating what to say. "One of the *weres* recognized me," he admitted.

This wasn't good news. I swallowed hard. "If they know you, they'll try to kill you, won't they?"

"Ordinarily, I'd agree. But I think they plan to keep me and Mother alive. As *weres,* our kind provides longer, more satisfying feeds. Vampires can drink from us for months, possibly even years, as we replenish our blood supply quicker. Since we can also regrow limbs, they'll sever our arms and legs for meat to feed the demons—"

"I'm going to stop you right there, big guy." Horror ripped through me. This couldn't be happening.

Sets of heavy footsteps echoed down from a row of nearby stairs. "Shit, grab 'em," someone growled as shrieks and frantic flapping ensued.

"God*damn*it!" another yelled.

What sounded like cage doors were slammed shut. "Get them upstairs and load them up with the others. They should be satisfied by now."

Metal rattled and someone grunted. "Grab the other end," yet another Tribesman muttered. "I don't want to get bit."

The crazed flapping and shrieking from the demon children seemed to fade as a few pairs of feet hurried up the creaky wooden steps. But the Tribesmen weren't all gone, and those who remained gathered at the bars in front of us.

A *were* in really ugly flannel rubbed his arm where one of the demon children had taken a chunk. But it was the vamp with the lengthening incisors who spoke. "Well, well, well. Looks like sleeping beauty is finally awake."

Gem snarled, positioning himself directly in front of me. I screamed when the vamp lifted his gun and fired. The shot struck Gem in the stomach, its force hurtling him back against the wall. The Tribesmen swarmed in, three shoving him back as he fought to return to where I lay.

"Get away from him," I shrieked. "Don't you touch him!"

The two vamps standing before me reached for the snaps on their jeans and shoved their waistbands down past their hips. "You should be more worried about yourself, cutie," one of them said.

Gem went ballistic, shoving his way forward. I didn't move, watching, waiting, and focusing, allowing the vamp to reach for the front of my dress before I exploded with fire and set him ablaze.

My magic was hindered with my hands tied behind me. But flame and light could still protect me and encase me with its power.

The vamp lit up like a torch and exploded—spraying us with his dusty remains. I choked on ash as his buddies slid over his leftovers, falling over each other in their mad scramble out.

Gem rolled forward, desperate to reach me. But I was blind to anything but the fleeing vamps.

My breath released in pained bursts. They were going to rape me. I should have been scared out of my mind, but only fury reigned, knowing how bad they'd hurt my wolf.

The vamp hoisting his jeans up hissed through the bars. "Just as well," he spat. "I don't want the whore of a werewolf."

My glare trained on him. "At least he has a bat, not a light switch for a penis."

Gem's furious face lessened in severity. "Taran—"

"Keep talking, you ball-less bastard," I snapped. "You'll never be the stud he is in bed."

"Taran—"

I motioned to Gem's lap. "You think he's hung now; you should see him when I work that log—"

"Taran!"

"What, babe?" I asked, getting annoyed. I was on a roll, and these idiots deserved far worse than my words.

He spoke through gritted teeth. "My parents can hear you."

Oh, yeah . . . them.

Oops.

From the other side of the wall, Pop muttered something in Japanese. Whatever it was turned Gem's pale face crimson.

The vamp hadn't appreciated the penile belittling and bashing of his boys. A sinful grin lit his face. "The lead demon child hasn't had his fill. But maybe the old ones will satisfy his needs."

My eyes widened as the vamps disappeared from sight. Gemini waited for their quick steps to bound up the stairs, and for a metal door to slam shut, before speaking fast. "Taran. Use your fire to burn through my restraints."

"I can't. With my hands bound I can only surround myself with fire. To generate enough heat to melt the restraints, I'll burn you."

"Don't worry about me—I'll heal." When he sensed my hesitation, his voice lowered to more of a plea. "Taran, it's the only way we'll get out alive."

About every swear word I knew spouted from my lips. I didn't want to hurt him, but I also didn't want us to die. "Get your hands behind mine," I managed.

I drew several breaths as he positioned his back against mine. "Can you see where my hands are?"

He squirmed against me. "Yes."

I extended my finger. "Put the center of the chain against it." The moment I felt the metal slide against my skin, I bent my knuckle around it. "Okay. Here goes."

I focused my energy on the links and took a deep breath, forcing my surrounding flame to slide along my skin and move toward my hands. Something sparked, causing Gem to grunt and jump. Nausea dug a hole in my belly as the smell of his smoking skin filled my nose. I cringed, trying not to gag. "Oh, God. Are you all right?"

He gasped as I withdrew my power. "Your fire is building and expanding outward. Can you keep it centered on the links?"

My head slumped forward. "I'm trying. But the longer it burns, the more it expands."

"What about pinching it between your fingers."

"I can try." I adjusted my body so I could reach the chain and secure it with my thumb and finger. He bit back a growl, but unlike before, I could feel the metal begin to melt within my grasp.

My fingers felt close to joining when the metal door opened with a bang and heavy clawed feet scraped along the steps. What sounded like a mammoth tail slapped against the wooden stairs until it reached the floor below and dragged along the concrete.

The lead demon had come to feast.

My heart thumped against my chest as I panicked—knowing I wouldn't be done in time to help Gem's parents. The image of their cold scowls faded, replaced with one of fear in their eyes and horror etched into their wrinkled features when the demon lurched forward and took his first bite.

Angry and frightened tears leaked from my eyes. I couldn't allow his parents to be eaten—I didn't want Momma and Pop to die!

"Taran, calm down and focus. You need to finish, love."

The cell door beside us was thrown open and a throaty, wet growl filled my ears. Moist splatters peppered the cement like rain. The demon was hungry, drool dripping from his voracious mouth. For a moment he seemed to watch, taking in the feast before him. But then from one breath to the next, he attacked.

Large wings flapped and the floor shook as the demon shot forward. They were going to die—they were going to be eaten—they—

I forced the heat to increase between my fingers, burning myself when my power rebounded.

"Taran, *stop,*" Gem growled through clenched teeth. "I don't want you hurt!"

"But your parents—"

Flying demon innards smacking against the far wall and sliding against the cinder block completely shut me up. The demon's entrails slithered into our cell like wet snakes, before drying near my bare feet. I gagged, but somehow managed to keep from vomiting.

Gem's shoulders slumped. "Taran," he said patiently. "My mother may be elderly, but she's still a werewolf."

"Ah . . . right."

I blinked back my remaining tears and shook my head to clear it. With a determined breath, I focused hard, gathering my flame. It took some doing, and a lot more supernatural muscle, but finally Gem grunted and broke through the dissolving links.

He snapped the cuffs from his wrists and the shackles binding his feet, flinging each to the side, and far from his body. His form shuddered with relief from the loss of gold, but also with weakness. My wolf wasn't doing so hot. Yet he steeled himself, gripped the choker tight, and ripped it down the center.

He swayed from the effort but forced himself to work fast, stripping me of my binds and wrenching me to my feet. My hands throbbed from the burn I'd caused, but I was still in better shape than my lover. I rubbed my sore wrists, watching the trickles of sweat stream down Gem's back as he kicked open the door to the cell.

We raced into the hall, our bare feet crunching over dry demon parts, and into the next cell. Gem's parents were bound but unharmed, wearing the same stone-faced expressions as always.

Evidently, they liked the idea of being demon food about as much as they liked me.

I jumped when Momma spat a large chunk of something

nasty near my feet. "Larynx," Gem said, pointing. "And probably part of a jugular."

I looked from the shriveling mound back at her, and back at the nastiness again. "Your mother ripped out his throat with her human teeth?"

Considering her unflinching scowl, Momma seemed quite proud of herself then. Instead of answering me, Gem beckoned the beast within him.

His twin ripped from his back, positioning himself to guard as Gem freed his folks. I glanced around their cell, my eyes latching onto a small window. Just beneath it lay an empty utility bucket. I kicked it over and stood on it, looking out to a frozen dirt lot with a large stretch of forest running along its perimeter. Feet hurried past me as Tribesmen carried cages packed with demon children onto the back of a large freight truck.

Gem hurried to where I stood, his gaze taking everything in. "Do you know where we are?" I asked.

He took a breath. "North of Tahoe from what I can tell, but I can't be certain." He huffed. "There are too many of them, and not enough of us. I'll draw their fire. You and my parents get to the woods and head south. Don't worry about me. I won't be far behind."

My magic sparked as my stare locked onto the screeching demon children being loaded like freaky livestock. As much as I wanted to live, we couldn't just run. They were being transported to their next safe haven to feed from and breed with innocent women.

I turned to Gem, my hands crackling with blue and white flames. "Uh, uh, uh, babe. No one draws fire like me . . ."

15

We made our way up the stairs, where Gem listened closely. The entire haven was bustling with activity, but it seemed to be directed outside.

"I don't like this," Gem muttered.

"You said yourself we need a distraction and that we're outnumbered," I whispered tightly.

"Which is why I should lead this attack," he snarled.

I snarled back, or at least I tried to. But all I managed was to drool on Pop's shoulder. I wiped it with my nasty hands and went all Jersey on my wolf. "Fine. Lead it. But if you want a diversion, I can make a lot more noise."

"Taran—" Gem started, but he was cut off by his father, who began to argue with him in Japanese. Gem barked back, furious.

Momma frowned my way. "How do you plan to distract them?"

It was Gem who answered for me. "She means to summon sunlight born of magic."

Oh, and didn't I have his parents' attention then? Pop narrowed his eyes. "You can do this?"

I nodded. "Yes."

Momma eyed me up and down. If it were possible, her scrutiny of me was more severe than, like, ever.

Vamps, demons, and demon children were immune to the sunshine. But sunlight born of magic was considered "pure" light and its power would burn them to ash. A gal like me capable of something pure? Yeah, I was. It shocked many. Including Momma. Hey, including me.

"But you are not a witch," she said slowly.

"Which is why it will leave her weak and vulnerable," Gemini said. His stare darkened. "I can't ask this of you."

"You're not asking," I said. "But I am telling you I'm going to do this."

Gemini's parents spoke quickly in Japanese. Gem shook his head slowly, clearly disagreeing with what they were saying. I couldn't understand a word and it pissed me off.

"If you're going to talk about me, at least say what you have to say in a language I can understand."

Gem's folks stared at me like I'd struck them with lightning, but Gem kept his expression hard. "They have guns, and weapons, and numbers we do not have on our side. I don't want to lose you."

"I don't want to lose you, either," I said, my voice shaking. "Any of you. So, let me try."

"No," Gem answered.

Pop spoke low and rough, but there was a softness to it I hadn't known. "You will lose each other if you do not let your mate help us, Tomo."

Yeah. We were pretty screwed. I was a tough girl, but it was hard to be tough knowing this could be goodbye. "Just clear me a path to the truck, and trust me to do the rest—"

I meant to say more, that I was sorry for all the royal screwups and that it had been my honor to meet them. Most of all, I wanted to thank Gemini for loving me. But all the kind words I meant to share lodged in my throat when a vampire wrenched open the door.

Gem's twin wolf lurched forward, decapitating the vamp in one bite. His human half exploded in wolf form, leaping over the remains and speeding ahead. There was a scream and the blast of a shotgun, and Christ in heaven it scared the life out of me. But now was no time to hide.

His parents and I scrambled forward into an old kitchen in time to see my wolves dive through the windows on either side of the door.

More gunshots, more screaming—Gem was taking on the entire camp alone! The kitchen door burst into splinters and several armed *weres* rushed in. Pop dove on top of me, forcing me to the floor. I couldn't see anything, but I heard more than I wanted to know.

Growls erupted and a barrage of bullets zipped over us, busting holes into the walls and doors and raining chunks of plaster and wood around us. I lay across the warped floor, covering my head, terrified it was over before it could actually start, until Pop's weight abruptly lifted.

Only the distant sounds filled the kitchen. I peered up to find a pure white wolf with a black streak down her back covered in blood and panting with excitement. She bounded over the carnage of dead *weres*, disappearing outside the door in fewer than two strides.

I rose slowly, trying to step around the bleeding corpses and severed heads. *"Taran,"* Pop urged.

I startled. Pop stood before me with two assault rifles strapped to his back and holding a third, while his free hand pointed to the open oven. "Distraction," he said.

Between Momma going all psycho and Pop ready to take on the Terminator, I have to admit, I needed a moment. Yet considering the air of death in the kitchen was quickly being replaced with the reek of gas, it wasn't a very long moment.

I nodded like an imbecile and hurried forward, sliding over a pool of blood, and of course swearing, since that's how I rolled. "Yay, team," I muttered.

I gathered my power, keeping it within my core as I stumbled forward. "Go," I told him. He didn't move right away. "Go, *fast*," I warned, my body shaking from the strength it took to maintain the growing inferno.

He nodded and ran out the door. I ran after him, unleashing a stream of blue and white right at the open oven door—

Oh, fuuuck.

The force of the blast launched me away from the house like a torpedo. Celia would have leapt out majestically, landing in a graceful crouch, and hit the ground in a mad dash.

Yeah. I so wasn't Celia.

My limbs flailed wildly as the earth sped past beneath me. It wasn't a conscious thought to gather my flame around me; it was more like pure instinct and the crazy desire to live. Blue and white cocooned me, shielding me from the explosion and the blazes shooting out in all directions.

To anyone passing, the scene probably looked badass, but there was nothing badass about my landing. Like a meteor striking the earth, I plowed across the lot, melting the snow and charring the earth beneath me.

I pushed up on my elbow, spitting out dirt and dumbstruck that I was still alive. I poked my head out of the large crater my crash had created and swore yet again.

In blurs of white and black, Gemini's wolves, and that of his mother, ripped into the vampires, blood streaming from jowls and soaking their furs. The house burned and smoked as blue and white flames ate through the walls and frame. The intense heat warmed my face from where I crouched, and I was a long way back!

At first, I thought it was a good thing—to destroy a place

where so many had suffered. Except neither Pop nor I had counted on the effects it would have on the demon children.

They lost their damn minds, rocking the freight truck with enough force to bounce the wheels. One flew out, flapping, desperate to escape, only to explode to bits of quivering maggots when Pop aimed and fired. Another followed, and another. Pop killed the second, but only clipped the wing of the third.

They were breaking out. We were out of time.

I crawled out of the hole and ran to where Pop used the butt of his remaining rifle to crush the demon's skull.

My arms electrified with energy as I flung mini-bolts from my hands, singeing anyone in my path. I needed to get to Pop. He was human, alone, and quickly running out of protection.

My hands scissored out as two *weres* charged me from both sides. The force of my lightning rammed their massive chests hard, flinging them backward to jerk and twitch along the ground. They weren't dead, but they were hurt. Yet I didn't have time to make the kill. Not if I wanted to save Pop.

With screams and swears, I released more lightning. The air crackled and charged as a darkening blue ray cut through the chest of a werebear and into the vamp aiming for Pop's head. Pop tossed his empty rifle and ran to pick up the one the vamp discarded upon his re-death. But Pop wasn't the only one in trouble. I sent an extra-large bolt into the vamp who had taken Momma to the ground. That one I killed, seconds before he would have snapped her neck, sending him airborne and into the burning house.

More Tribesmen bounded for me before I was halfway across the lot. Gem's twin took on three. I took on the rest. My fire detonated skulls and seared through bellies, mostly by luck. I didn't aim; there was no time really. I was just trying to keep from being eaten and ripped apart.

As I ran, I watched Pop fire at more fleeing demon children.

He managed to hit each one, but even from a distance, I could sense his exhaustion, just as I could see the demon children were moments from tipping the entire truck on its side.

Tears streamed down my face as my bare feet met the bitter sting of the frigid snow and sharp gravel. I didn't have the tough hide of Celia, or the ability to heal myself like Emme, nor did I possess Shayna's fighting skills. I was just me.

But maybe I was just what we needed.

The fury of war surrounded me as Tribesmen cocked their weapons and fired. I couldn't spare the magic I needed, but I also couldn't die. I dove to the ground and curled inward, using my fire as a shield. Bullets sprayed against my body, bursting into small poofs of ash as my flame ignited them.

I couldn't see anything. But when I heard Gem's howl, and Pop urging me forward, I leapt up in a burst of speed and light. I tore through the last remaining feet separating me from the truck. My gasps of breath were visible in the frigid air, and my thighs burned. I was already worn out. But Momma's pained yelp forced me to act.

I closed my eyes, ignoring the chaos around me, focusing on my inner light, the one that triggered my power, and the only thing pure about me. As I concentrated, it flickered to life and expanded, my breaths became more controlled, and my head lolled forward. *That's it. Give me more, baby.*

I was sure it would keep going. But unlike the times before, when I wasn't so beaten and raw, this time my power resisted, ignoring my pleas to surge forth.

My light dwindled and flared, sputtering close to either swelling or extinguishing the piddly amount I managed to stir, until my anger and frustration took over and riled it awake.

The light sparked, sizzled, and *burned,* stalling briefly over the distant whines of hurting beasts, and a yelp from a wolf I knew too well. I forced away all thoughts of pain, filling myself with the peace I'd sought for so long.

Slowly, my feet levitated from the ground. A small, wicked smile inched across my face. I had the light, to clutch, to harness, to kindle, allowing it to grow into a roaring beast of its own.

There was no stopping me now. I was now one with my light, a dangerous inferno begging to be released. My body spun and my power raged in tune with the terrified shrieking of the demon children. I opened my eyes in time to see a swarm of flapping bodies wiggle free of their cages, their beady red eyes trained on me.

Okay, boys, time to burn.

Light as pure as heaven erupted from my core in a sudden, mighty burst as an army of winged leathery bodies soared toward me with their fangs and claws exposed. The light, so beautiful and fierce, blinded me. I couldn't see, but I heard a shotgun blast exploding in front of me.

For all I worked for it, and for all I owned it then, the glorious brilliance abruptly faded, leaving me at once and dropping me against the hard ground.

The jolt from the impact should have been enough to force me to my feet, but it wasn't. My head weighed more than it should, and my muscles were nothing more than useless groupings of gelatin.

I was vaguely aware of Pop rushing to my side, but it was his heartbroken voice that latched to my brain and whispered a warning. "My *son,*" he said.

My eyes whipped open, and I forced myself up on my arms only to scream. I didn't care about the mountains of ash that had been vampires moments before, or about the empty cages and demon remains littering the truck floor and ground around me.

I didn't care that my magic had spared us. All I cared about was the naked body lying motionless before me.

"No!"

I crawled forward, pushing past the weakness and chills racking my body to roll Gem over and onto his back. A pained sob ripped through my throat. All I could do was scream. There, in the center of his chest, a gaping hole exposed where his heart had once beat and given him life.

He'd taken a bullet meant for me, sacrificing himself so I could live. He shouldn't have done that. He shouldn't have left me. Jesus *Christ*, why did he leave me?

I flung my arms around his neck and pulled him against my trembling form, my heaving breaths burning their way through my lungs.

He was dead, and despite all of my power, despite all my supposed gifts, there was nothing I could do. Instead of life, I begged for death then. For one vamp to have escaped my light, so I wouldn't know another moment without him.

"Taran," Momma whispered gently.

I ignored her, crying uncontrollably as Gemini's spilling blood grew cold against my skin. Pop hooked his arms undermine. "Come, Taran," he urged.

He tried to pull me away, but I wrenched free, drawing Gemini closer, refusing to let go. "Get off me!" I shrieked. "I won't leave him!"

My sobs morphed into hysteria, and my grip around Gem tightened. Gem's parents tried to speak to me, but I barely heard them over my cries and didn't care enough to listen.

It took a small and poignant whine to snag my attention and pull me toward its source.

Before me stood Gem's other wolf half. Although I froze, I couldn't control the whimpering that ensued.

"Taran," Momma said softly. "You must release Tomo so his other wolf can return to his body and heal him."

"He didn't die, too?" I stammered. It was a stupid question, seeing as he stood in front of me. I just thought . . . I thought . . .

When I remained unmoving, Pop reached for me again.

This time, I allowed him to ease me away. My hands released Gemini carefully, despite the numbness dulling my heartbeat to painful thuds.

As I watched, Gemini's twin wolf limped forward and merged with his human half. Gem jerked up into a sitting position, coughing and grunting, his large hand pressed tight against his chest. Agony twisted his features and perspiration released in streams down his face. His features relaxed with each breath, until he was finally able to pry his eyes open and latch them onto mine.

I flung myself on top of him and showed him love the only way I knew how.

"Motherfucking, dipshit, fuck-loving whore. Don't you *ever* do that to me again!"

I might have said more. Mostly I just cried.

Despite Momma's and Pop's audible gasps, and our current situation, Gemini pulled me close and chuckled against my ear. "I love you, too," he murmured.

16

Gemini held me, until a cougar in beast form stirred in front of us. Pop shot it, the bullet striking his hide, but since he missed his skull and heart by a mile, the *were* didn't die. Pop mumbled something in Japanese and tossed his last rifle aside. Mom barreled forward in her wolf form, ripping into the cougar and killing it.

The moment she dropped the cougar's limp form, her head whipped in the direction of a road. She growled and yipped. Pop stripped out of his dress shirt and passed it to Gem. Gem quickly tied the shirt his father had given him into a makeshift loincloth. "More are coming," Gem said. "We have to leave now."

A few feet from us, more *weres* began to stir. I nodded, knowing he was right, but that was all I could do. I slumped to my side and into a pile of leftover demon bits.

My sunlight born of magic obliterated all the vamps and demon children in the vicinity, but it had no affect on the *weres*. They were waking, healing, struggling to rise. And although I couldn't hear any vehicles approaching, Momma's increasing yips warned something else was closing in.

She dashed forward, allowing Pop to climb on her furry and blood-smeared back. She waited for Gemini to wrench me into his arms before taking off in a mad sprint and disappearing into the dense forest.

I couldn't have ridden him as wolf. The magic I used to produce the sunlight left me debilitated. "Call the pack," I mumbled. "We need help."

"I did, Taran. But that's not them coming." The branches slapped against his arms. "We're too far in enemy territory. Our only choice is to run."

"The fire," I rasped. "They'll see my fire and know."

"Maybe. But we can't wait for them to arrive."

I tried to say more but failed, my body appearing to sink inward. I slumped against Gem's chest, vaguely aware something was off in the way he ran, before I closed my eyes and surrendered to my exhaustion.

I don't remember sleeping. There were moments I'd wake only to be lulled back to sleep by the motion with which Gem carried me. What I remembered was the moon. The sun was shining high above us when we made our escape. Now, only night reigned. I remember thinking I should eat, or drink, or speak before fatigue gripped me and my eyelids drooped once more.

The next time I opened my eyes, the dull light of the autumn sun greeted me on the horizon.

"Gem," I whispered, rubbing the sleep from my eyes. "Where are we?"

"Close," he answered, his voice oddly choked.

I lifted my chin, my eyes widening. The sunlight beat against his face. But instead of bronzing his olive skin and enveloping it in its welcoming glow, it cast a spotlight on skin as white as bleached wood. I reached and stroked his sweat-soaked cheek, his skin so cold and drained of color I didn't know how he could stand, much less run.

"Baby . . ." I began, but my breath lodged in my throat. Gem was so pale, and the circles ringing his eyes were so dark, he was almost unrecognizable.

"Baby, stop."

Sweat poured down his face. "No," he panted. "We're close to Tahoe. I can sense its energy."

"Then *call* to the pack—or put me down. Jesus, you look like death."

"Still too far to be heard by our friends, and too close to our enemies," he bit out. "I need to get us closer to call for help."

I craned my neck enough to see his mother racing in her wolf form beside us. Her stare remained focused ahead, but his father managed to toss me a glance. Worry creased his brow. I thought he nodded in agreement with me, or maybe I only imagined it. I muttered about six more swear words, which did nothing of course. *Damn.* I felt so helpless!

Gemini continued to move fast, but his speed was significantly slower than I remembered it. I'd known him to run all night and into the dawn with only determination fixed in those dark eyes. Now, all I saw was excruciating pain twisting his features. Perspiration cut lines down his face and his breath released in quick, labored bursts. His condition wasn't due to exhaustion. My wolf was sick. Really sick.

"Is it your heart?" I managed, fearing the worst.

"No."

"Then what's happening?"

His skin alternated in shades of white. "I just need to keep going," was all he'd say.

I wriggled in his arms. "Put me down. I'll walk. You can't keep carrying me in your state."

"*No.*"

"Gem—"

"You can't walk with bare feet on this terrain, much less run as fast as me. I don't know how close the Tribesmen are." He swallowed, struggling to form his words. "What I do know is we need more miles between us and them."

It was hurting him even to speak, so for once in my life I didn't argue and shut my trap. My hands linked around his neck and I simply held him, trying to give him the strength I'd replenished during sleep, though I knew that wasn't possible. For all the magic I possessed, I could do nothing to spare him from his pain.

I closed my eyes, struggling to stay strong. *Don't cry. He needs a fighter, not some whiner,* my mind insisted.

I don't know how much longer he ran—an hour? Maybe more. I only remember the pine branches slapping and whipping Gem's arms seconds before we broke through the brush and into a wide clearing.

Gem stumbled onto his knees, grunting when he landed on a cluster of flat rocks, trying to protect my body from falling forward. I would rather have taken the brunt. If anything, he'd damaged his body worse than it already was. I kissed his cheek. "I'm okay. Let me go."

At first, he wouldn't ease his hold. It was almost as if he couldn't hear or didn't understand. Slowly, he released me, keeping his position as I hurried to stand. I lost my footing, my muscles tight and stiff from being carried so long and landed on my ass. Gem reached to steady me when I tried to stand, despite his slumping form and blatant pain.

"I'm fine, baby," I insisted.

I ignored the fiery sting as my bare feet stomped across the ground and huddled against the blistering wind, drawing enough fire around me to heat my legs and help me stagger to Gem's side. God, he appeared seconds from keeling over.

His father left his mother's back, the poor man crawling to Gem's side. Unlike me, he hadn't slept, the night's ride taking its toll on his age and his battered body. I reached for him, but he shook his head. "My son," he stammered.

Momma circled in her beast form keeping guard, but she was also racked with fear.

"We're not far," Gem spat. He'd repeated the words like he hadn't said them before. I think he meant to reassure us, but his condition was nothing short of unbridled suffering.

He swiveled his head from side to side, scrunching his face, kneeling with his hands out in front of him. That familiar sound of Velcro tearing filled my ears as his twin wolf's head punched through his back and broke free of his shelter.

Gem's body buckled when his wolf's hind legs hit the ground. I'd barely managed to put out my fire and curl my body around his in time. I dove to protect his head, its weight crushing my forearms and my motions scraping my arms along the rough terrain.

He lay there, with wide, unblinking eyes. If it weren't for the large gulps of air he was taking, I don't think he would've moved at all.

The separation from his wolf morphed his skin tone from alabaster white to a nausea-inducing gray. That was bad enough, but when his large beast collapsed beside him, I couldn't help but scream.

I clutched Gem's head, bringing it to my lap and reaching out to stroke his wolf. My fingers passed along his dense fur, his skin feeling cold against my touch. The beast panted heavily beside me, his dull eyes lacking the strength that warned those who dared to cross his path.

"Get up," Gem grunted through his teeth.

The wolf whined and twitched his muscles, every torturous movement clenching my lungs and robbing me of air. "Babe, don't." I shook my head. "Please. He's hurting, too."

Gem ignored me. *"Get up,"* he growled. "She needs you."

I wiped the tear I allowed to escape as I watched the wolf struggle to rise. He swayed more than once, yet somehow manage to keep his feet. Gem's brow cooled beneath my touch.

"You need him back inside you," I stammered. "Please don't make him go."

"We're close," Gem slurred, dragging out his next few words. "We can feel them."

My body shuddered with cold and every emotion raking down to my core. "You're not going to make it, love. Not if he goes."

"None of us will make it if he doesn't. Go," he whispered, his breaths so shallow they were barely visible in the cold air.

The wolf met my eyes briefly before he limped across the clearing and back into the forest. As he disappeared, I watched my lover fade into darkness.

Some women could cry, and cry, and cry, allowing those around them to coddle them and surround them with their strength while they did nothing more than unleash their grief. Sure, there were moments when they should: a death, a fatal diagnosis, a severe illness, or uncontrollable pain.

But I didn't have the luxury of tears, or the help of others. Instead of crying like I would've preferred, and hated myself for later, I acted.

I kissed Gem's shoulder and motioned his father closer. "Stay with him; keep him warm with your body. I'll gather wood to start a fire." To his mother I said, "Guard them—I won't be long."

Momma stopped pacing, appearing to frown.

"No fire, Taran. The Tribe will find us," Pop insisted.

"Our friends will find us dead if I don't." I motioned to Gem. "Just do what I ask. *Please.*"

His eyes widened at my desperation, and he exchanged glances with his wolf wife before crawling forward and huddling around his son. "Branches are too wet or too green," he muttered. "They won't burn."

I rose, my numbing feet throbbing with each step. "I'll make them burn," I assured him.

Flames sizzled above my head. Their intensity so fierce I barely heard the howl of the increasing wind over their hiss. It wasn't intentional. I hadn't called forth that power. I was simply that livid. I wouldn't go down like this—in the woods, barefoot, half-naked—especially this close to salvation.

And neither would Gemini.

I stomped my feet, forcing fire to engulf my soles and ribbon my legs and thighs. I lifted my arms out. With a swoosh, my hands and forearms followed in a blaze of light.

Warmth wound along my extended limbs, reminding me just how cold the rest of me was. I shuddered and moved forward, my aching bones creaking in protest.

"Shut up," I told them. "You're acting like a bunch of bitches." I cringed when Pop abruptly stopped speaking. I glanced over my shoulder, only to meet Gem's parents' stunned faces. "Not you. I meant my bones—*bones*." With a defeated sigh I plowed forward. Would I *ever* get anything right with them?

Snow melted beneath my feet with each step I managed, my frustration burning an imprint down to the soil. I wasn't stupid. I knew I was all but mapping out our location. But Gem couldn't wait in the cold, not in his condition.

I shook out the flames in my hands as I neared the long stretch of trees and reached for what I thought was a branch buried in the snow. FYI, it was a root. And FYI, I landed on my ass again.

I had to surround myself in flame just to warm up again before I caught sight of a chunk of log. It wasn't that big, but it would hopefully hold us over. I dragged it along the ground, my face scrunching from the splintering wood digging into my skin, yelling and of course swearing in the process. Thankfully, the only attention it drew was Momma's. She bounded over the snow and raced to my side, lifting the piece in her powerful jaws with the same effort most would lift an empty box. I nodded. "Okay, girl, remind me never to piss you off." It was a stupid thing to say considering I'd flung her down a mountain.

I couldn't be sure, but she might have grinned. She didn't wait for me, though, and trotted off with the large chunk of wood in her mouth. My gifts included the ability to strut in four-inch platforms across a layer of gravel. But this wasn't gravel, and my feet were bare. I stumbled, cursed some more, and wobbled my way back to them. I didn't think I'd wandered far, but it seemed far just then.

In the time it took me to return, Momma Hamamatsu had dug out a small circle in the dirt and dropped the log dead center. Gemini lay unmoving, with his father's small body trembling uncontrollably as he curled against his son. My need to warm them and the emotion the scene evoked made me careless. I concentrated my power into my palm and flung a softball-sized sphere at the log . . . which grew in size with each rotation.

"Son of a *bitch*!"

Momma soared across the space between the log and her family, shielding them with her massive body as my flaming ball struck the log in an angry burst. The log fired, spitting flames and roaring in a scorching F-you blaze.

I jetted toward them, falling more than once. Momma's eyes narrowed as I batted out her fur with my hands, withdrawing the blue and white tendrils with each strike. "God, I'm, like, so sorry."

She sneezed, likely because of all the singed fur drifting in the air as my hands continued to slap mercilessly against her hide. I coughed and gagged when some strands tickled the back of my throat. "Damn it. This shit's everywhere."

Believe it or not, it was more of a jab at me for my carelessness than anything directed at Gem's mother. Of course, Momma didn't take it that way. Her dark wolf eyes regarded me as if she'd like nothing more than to rip out my throat and roast my ass for breakfast.

Gem's father poked his head out from her other side when the flames dwindled down to a respectable fire. He looked from me to the hairless patches of skin spreading along his mate's body. I petted a particularly large bald spot. "I'm sure it'll grow back." *Maybe.* My fire generally had a freaky effect on preternaturals.

My shoulders slumped the longer they scrutinized me. If so much as a toe had stepped onto the Taran Bandwagon, I'm sure that toe had leapt off so their bodies could moon me as the wagon sped off. "Sorry?" I offered.

Gem's dad deepened his scowl. "Tomo needs food."

Momma rose slowly and shook off more damaged fur. Girlfriend wasn't looking so hot, but her son was much worse. I gathered him to me, trying to keep his body warm with mine.

Momma sat on her hind legs and closed her eyes, her large nose flaring until something caught her attention and she took off into the brush. I waited for her to disappear before speaking, careful to take in our surroundings. "Why don't you sleep?" I told Pop. "I'll stand guard."

He seemed to hesitate. My hand passed along Gemini's spine. "I've slept. You haven't," I pointed out.

"The magic you drew was powerful."

I shrugged. "I s'pose."

His face tightened. "You're not weak?"

He wasn't *were,* but something in the way he carried himself told me he could sense a lie as easily as his wife. This man had experienced a lot in his life. "I am a little weak still. What helps me most is sleep, which your son made sure I had." I pressed a kiss on Gem's bare shoulder. "I can fight if I need to. And I will. I swear it."

That much I meant. My protective instincts and will to survive were officially in overdrive. If anything was stupid enough to approach us then, I'd likely set this whole forest aflame.

My response seemed to satisfy him. Pop staggered to his feet, hugging his body, and shuffled closer to the fire. Gem squirmed beneath my touch, struggling to inch closer. My lips found his, and my thumb brushed over the skin beside his ear. He couldn't see how bad he looked, but I'm sure he felt it. "Do you want me to adjust your position?" I asked.

"No. The heat feels good on my back."

He sounded so weak, and it scared me. "What's happening to you?"

It seemed to hurt him to speak, but it also seemed like he needed to tell me. "The bullets have gold in them."

My lips parted. "But the shells were silver."

He kept his eyes closed but continued to speak. "They were encased in silver, but I can feel the gold within them." He swallowed hard. "The silver alloy protects the fragments of gold, fooling my body into healing around them."

My eyes widened. This wasn't good. This wasn't good at all. "Gem, I need you to be honest with me. . .How many times were you shot?"

His head lolled to the side. "At least six. Maybe more."

Tears blurred my vision as it became clear what was happening. His healing abilities had betrayed him and cocooned the gold within his body. Had all the bullets been all gold, they'd burn the tissue around them, preventing it from fully healing, all the while poisoning his bloodstream. But those would be easy to locate. Aric had once been shot full of gold and had pushed the bullets out through his skin with a screwdriver.

I tried not to think what awaited Gemini if help didn't arrive soon. These bullets within him might have been cheaper than actual cursed gold, but they were effective. I couldn't push or burn them out. I couldn't do anything with his body trapping and hiding them from us.

I took a few breaths to steady my mounting fury and keep my power in check. "They'll have to be dug out, won't they?"

I thought he'd fallen asleep until he answered. "Yes."

"And your heart?"

"The bullet detonated part of my heart, but that's a good thing," he slurred.

"You have to be kidding me."

"The fragments spread along my chest when it exploded," he said, his words slow and hard to understand. "Away from what remained of my heart, allowing my other wolf to heal the part that was spared . . . Otherwise, I wouldn't have made it."

It was great news in a way. Yet as I pictured fragments of metal scattered along his chest cavity, let's just say the nurse in me was grateful to be horizontal at that moment. "You need Emme," I said quietly.

"No. Emme's power will further encase the bullets within me." He lifted his heavy eyelids. "I need Shayna. She'll be able to sense where the metal is. Either she or Celia could dig them out. My brothers won't be able to without feeling the effects."

"Celia will do it. Her hands are steady, and she can disconnect and focus better than the others."

I didn't need to add that Shayna and Emme were more emotional. Or that I was, too, when it came to my wolf. I sniffled a little. There was a reason Celia was our rock. Although she felt very deeply, when we needed her strength, it never faltered. "She'll make it right," I promised.

17

I spent the remainder of the day feeding Gem chunks of ice, in addition to pieces of rabbit, squirrel, and something that resembled a possum. Momma had hooked us up big time. I ate, mostly to keep my strength up, and not because I felt like eating.

Around noon Gem told us his twin was close to finding our friends. I didn't remind him that he'd said the same thing at the crack of dawn. He knew as much, and my complaining wouldn't help him. I hoped the nourishment he received would help him rise so we could trek our way through the forest and closer to civilization, but without his other wolf, he could barely harness enough energy to eat.

Close to dusk, something riled Momma's wolf. She leapt to her feet, her spine and tail so stiff Pop and I scrambled to stand, expecting the worse. Lightning zapped from my fingertips, sending the fine hairs on my arms to stand on end. My nerves were so on edge, sparks scattered along the frozen earth.

I waited. And I was glad I did. Through the stretch of dense vegetation and darkness, I caught my first view of big Jersey hair. "Here!" Celia called behind her. "I found them."

Celia shot forward, her tigress eyes flashing briefly in the fire's glow. I almost broke down when she snatched me in her arms, but her embrace wasn't what I needed. She realized as much before I could break free and fell to Gemini's side, dropping the pack she carried beside him.

She nudged his shoulder carefully. "Gem, can you hear me?" She glanced up when he failed to answer. "How long has he been unconscious?"

My voice shook. "I don't know—a few hours. He was in and out, but then he just seemed to fade."

She unzipped her pack and fumbled through the contents. "I have clothes."

"I'll do it," I snapped. I didn't mean to react the way I did, and I'm not sure where the response came from. Thankfully, Celia didn't appear to take offense. Without so much as blinking, she passed me a thick pair of sweatpants. "Sorry. I'm tired . . . and angry . . . and-and . . ." I tripped over my last few words.

When she squeezed my shoulder, I thought I would lose it. "It's okay. It's a mate thing," she said quietly.

It was as if she'd slapped me across the face with a chunk of bear liver. "What?" I dragged the pants along his legs, struggling against their dead weight.

Celia met me with kindness. "Your need to protect your mate is overtaking your reason," she said. "Remember how crazy Koda acted if anyone approached Shayna after she was hurt?"

"Crazy" was putting it lightly. I considered slapping on a muzzle oh him.

"I don't mean to be a prick," I admitted.

Celia turned from passing Pop a garbage bag stuffed to the brim with what appeared to be more clothes. Despite the fire, we were freezing our asses off. Yet Pop's hands stopped in the process of tearing open the bag to scowl at me.

"I meant no offense to your manhood," I added apologetically.

Celia grimaced, making it clear it was time to stop talking. She motioned to Gem. "Are you okay if I put socks on his feet?"

I had built up a sweat just hauling the waistband up to his thighs. It was nuts—and I didn't want to admit it—but it was like Celia said I couldn't handle another female touching him.

Don't be an asshole, I told myself.

At my nod, she hurried to slip his socks on. She'd only managed one when Koda, Liam, Emme, and Shayna arrived. They swept in like smoke. Relief should have flooded my system. Instead, all I could do was gasp.

Koda carried Gemini's twin draped across his shoulders. The large wolf was limp, his tongue lolling over his opened mouth. Celia seized me around the waist, clamping my wrists with her hands. "Taran, don't. It's okay, Taran. It's okay."

No. It wasn't.

I fought her hold, my body trembling, needing to erupt in flame.

Liam quickly lowered Emme to the floor, racing toward us. "Celia, get away from her!"

Shayna and Emme approached slowly with their hands out. "Don't do it, Taran," Emme urged. "Please calm down, honey."

"T, pull back your power," Shayna pleaded. *"Please.* You'll hurt Celia."

I grunted, the need to lash out pumping liquid fire through my veins. Celia held tight; her voice surprisingly steady. "She's okay, aren't you, Taran?"

I bowed my head, biting through the pain stabbing down to my gut. "Is he dead?" I asked through clenched teeth.

"No," Celia answered. "But he needs to merge with his other half. Let him, okay?"

She released me, following my half-assed nod.

Koda carefully lay the twin wolf beside his human half, but

kept a watchful eye on me, pulling Shayna far from my reach. He perceived me as volatile, unstable, and maybe more.

His perception was dead on.

"Go to him," Celia whispered.

I more or less moved to his side out of instinct, dread locking me in a haze. I collapsed near his head, where I could touch both wolf and man. Where Gem's breaths were barely visible, his wolf's seemed completely absent.

My fingers clutched the wolf's fur. I didn't believe he was alive, not then, until I caught the barest twitch of his nose. He blinked up at me with dead eyes yet managed to thump his tail when his gaze met mine.

"He likes me," I stammered. It was such an asinine thing to say, but it slipped out anyway, and caused my eyes to tear.

Celia's hand stroked my back. "No. He loves you, Taran."

My vision clouded with tears as my hand gently skimmed along his soft fur. "Time to go home," I told him. "He needs you, and I need you with him."

At my words, the wolf lifted his head, shimmying closer to Gemini. Ordinarily the union was a scene of beauty and awe. It wasn't beautiful then. Gem curled inward as his beast tried to push his way back inside him. Instead of accepting the unity, both seemed to fight it, Gem tensing and snarling in pain and his wolf whimpering and writhing.

I understood what was happening. But that didn't mean I liked it.

I snatched Emme's wrist when she extended her hands toward his shoulder. "Don't touch him."

"He needs help healing, Taran," Koda growled.

I understood his need to protect his friend. But Koda needed to stifle those growls. "There are bullets buried inside of him with gold at their centers," I snapped. "If she tries to heal him, they'll embed deeper into his tissue, muscles, and organs."

Koda tightened his stance. "How many bullets are we talking about?"

I watched the wolf collapse once more; certain I'd lose what remained of my sanity. "At least six, plus shards of metal in his chest cavity."

"Oh, hell," Liam said. He lifted Emme up and away from Gemini. "No wonder he's so sick."

Celia withdrew slightly and passed a thermos to Gem's dad. "It also explains why it's hurting his wolf to merge them."

"He needs to, though," Koda said. This time he kept his voice soft. "Gem will be stronger with him than without."

I continued to stroke Gem's twin as my eyes swam in a pool of my tears. "His heart was blown out. His twin healed him, but the shards are close to the regenerated muscle. We need to get these bullets out fast." I faced Celia; whose soul seemed to shatter in front of me. *Yeah. Join the club, sister.* "Will you do it?" I asked her.

She nodded. "Of course. We're about ten miles from the house. It will take us about half an hour to reach safety."

I passed my hand along the wolf's face. "Did you hear that? Thirty minutes. No more waiting. You need to get this done."

Once more he lifted his head. He shuffled his body along the frozen ground until his nose was an inch from Gem's back. With a deafening crunch and a heart-wrenching howl, Gem and his twin were whole once more.

I wiped my tears and turned to Shayna, who clasped her hands tight around her mouth, an expression of horror lining her pixie face. "I'm counting on you to find those bullets," I told her. "Don't let me down."

18

Okay. Fast-forward to the longest thirty minutes of my life. Towels were spread along our kitchen table. I'd wanted Celia to perform her surgery on our bed, but when Shayna started marking off the location of the bullets with a Sharpie, it became clear Celia would need more room to work.

God help me.

Emme dumped several of our utensils along the granite countertop. Celia pointed to a couple of spoons and several knives. "I need about four clamps, three scalpels, and three tweezers," she told Shayna. "You and Emme will need to pull the skin back. Make the handles long enough so you'll have a steady grip. His wolves may be sick, but they'll still try to heal him. Make the blades on the scalpels as thin and sharp as you can manage. Got me?"

My hands covered one of Gem's as he lay there. Just lay there. The merging of his twin had transformed his color from dark to light gray. At that point, I'd have given anything to have him return to the alabaster tone he'd had around dawn.

That color was a remarkable improvement to what I saw then.

Shayna went to work as Emme bolted around the kitchen filling bowls with water and collecting more towels. Celia approached me slowly and placed her hand tenderly on my shoulder. "How are you holding up?"

"I want to gut something evil and strangle it with its lower bowel," I answered truthfully. "If you screw this up, I might seriously burn the house down."

She blinked and patted my shoulder in a way that clearly demonstrated she doubted my stability just then.

In all fairness, I was feeling pretty psycho.

"She doesn't mean that," Emme assured the wolves. My glare told her I did. "Ah, but just in case, why don't you boys gather the fire extinguishers from each floor."

Koda took off right away. Liam started to follow but stopped to speak to Celia. Yet I wish to God and back he hadn't.

"Aric just texted," he told her. "His search party was out toward Nevada, so it's taking them a while to get back. But don't worry—he won't bring Barbara here, or have sex with her in front of you or anything."

Celia swallowed hard, clutching the scalpel she was inspecting tight in her hand. "Good to know," she managed.

Shayna threw her hands in the air. "Dude. Just get the extinguishers."

With my free hand, I smacked his arm as he passed. "What is *wrong* with you?"

Emme frowned, although I hadn't hurt him. "I know you're upset, but don't treat him that way."

As much as I wanted to lash out and tell her he deserved as much, I held back, knowing she was right. Liam was, at times, not the sharpest tool in the shed. But he wasn't mean. "Sorry," I muttered.

Liam considered me. "It's okay. I know you can't help being a bitch."

I should have added fire to that smack.

"Taran," Celia warned, when lightning sparked above my head.

"I'm not going to singe him," I promised, even though it was hard to hold back. I shook away my anger when it occurred to me there was more to worry about, meeting Celia with sympathy. "Are you going to be all right if Aric comes? —I'm serious. 'Cause if you're not, I need to tell him he can't come."

"As Gemini's alpha and his friend, Aric needs to be here," she answered.

"Ceel, you know that's not what I'm asking."

Her expression, while neutral, flickered with the barest trace of sadness. Her tone, though, remained even. "I swear to you, I'll do everything I can to help Gemini and get him through this. No matter who shows."

As everyone gathered around us, I hoped she was right. "Okay, Ceel. Get it done."

With a stiff nod she addressed the wolves. "Are you feeling the effects of the poison?"

Momma and Pop kept their die-hard poker faces, but it was Koda who spoke. "We can feel it, but we're okay." His eyes traveled to where Gem's parents watched. "Honorable parents, as third in command to Leader and pureblood Aric Connor of the Squaw Valley Den Pack, I respectfully request you keep a safe distance, and allow us to take over Tomo's care."

In other words, kindly move your asses.

It was Gemini's father who answered with a bow. Momma followed with a bow of her own, then went to sit beside her husband when he perched on a stool behind the raised counter. If Celia was fearful, she didn't show it. Instead, she leaned in to whisper in Gem's ear. "Okay, buddy. It's time. I'm not going to be gentle. But if you let me, I can help you."

His lips moved, but I couldn't hear him. Whatever he said widened Celia's eyes. She collected herself and edged closer to her tools. "What did he say?" I asked her.

"Nothing," she muttered, passing her hand along the makeshift surgical instruments.

A feeling of dread washed over me. "Celia, if this has something to do with Gemini, you need to tell me."

It was Koda who answered. He crossed his arms over his massive chest, his attention on Celia. "He swore that as his Leader's mate, he could never hurt her."

Celia shook off the comment like she hadn't been kicked in heart. Ordinarily, I would've been upset at Gemini for saying what he did. But just then, I only wanted him well.

"Koda, Liam," she called. "I need you to carefully roll Gemini onto his back."

Liam pointed. "But he's favoring his right side. Shouldn't we leave him on his left?"

"I need access to his chest," she answered.

Liam looked from me back to Celia. "Why?" he asked.

She gave me a dark look, her hand on something that resembled a hedge clipper. "I need to break open his chest cavity . . ."

E*ACH* *DING* into the ceramic bowl signified a fragment of metal or gold Celia dislodged from Gem's chest. Each threatened to stop my heart. Emme was sick more than once, and Shayna was looking pretty green as she ran out to dump the pieces. The wolves were sweating, grimacing each time Celia plucked another shard.

"The bullets don't just contain slivers of gold," Koda snarled. "The inner casing is lined with that shit."

I saw enough of one to know he was right.

Celia ignored everyone around her, working fast, almost

robotically. And thank God she could! Otherwise no way could she have stomached the crunch that followed when she snapped Gem's chest open at the sternum. Liam, for all his often inappropriate comments, held strong, keeping Gem's ribs apart so Celia could remove the biggest shard inches from Gemini's heart. Problem was, the cursed gold was starting to take its toll on all the wolves.

"Okay," Celia said, gasping. "Get him on his belly."

Everyone jumped when Liam released the ribs and they snapped back with a sickening crack. The wolves returned to Gemini slowly, waiting for the muscles and skin to knit closed before rolling him onto his stomach.

I wiped Gem's brow with a damp towel. Celia resumed her work, and another piece of metal hit the bowl. "Almost done, baby," I told him. "Three left."

My wolf, so ill and weak before, wasn't so ill and weak then. The next bullet Celia yanked forced his twin to punch his head through Gem's back, his snarling fangs snapping at Koda and Liam. Liam narrowly missed having his face chewed off.

At first the wolves had been patient, making animal sounds and using words to try to soothe Gemini's furious inner beasts. Problem was, Liam and Koda were dominant wolves in their own right. It wasn't long before their patience ran thin.

"Hold him!" Celia urged.

"We're *trying,*" Koda grunted, breathing hard. "Shayna, stay behind me—*Shayna.*"

In any other situation, no way would Gem ever think about hurting Shayna. But in his current state, he only felt agony, compelling his animal side to protect him from the pain. Shayna lurched back, poking her head from behind Koda when Gem's twin surfaced once more. "Ceel?" she asked as Celia discarded another extracted bullet from the tip of her instrument.

Celia waited for Gemini to lull his twin back to sleep. She

pointed near the center of his back as the wolf disappeared beneath his skin. "One more," she said.

A knock on the door froze everyone where they were, except for Gem, whose breathing was so harsh, his breaths lifted his upper body from the table.

Shayna rushed to the door when another knock, this one harder, quickly followed. She stole a glance at Celia before disappearing around the corner.

"Let's keep going," Celia said, lifting the scalpel and repositioning those hideous tweezers in her hands.

"You can do this, baby," I told Gem. "Almost done. I swear to God you're almost there."

The front door flung open as I spoke. "It's okay—he's hanging in, dude," she assured our latest visitor.

"Wait here unless you're *called*," Aric's voice ordered. Clearly, he hadn't come alone.

Heavy footsteps followed Shayna's light ones as they raced into the kitchen. The tension that followed Aric's arrival cloaked the room like the flash of a loaded gun. My grip to Gemini's shoulder tightened when he bit back a snarl. Celia, in her haste to help him, showed no mercy. In a way, I was grateful. In another not-so-great way, it made me want to ignite this kitchen in a wash of blue and white.

Gemini's growls rammed against my chest like a stake. Sweet God in heaven, how much more could my wolf take after having a portion of his heart blown to bits?

My chin jerked up when he bucked. Koda and Liam were practically lying across him, holding him down with their brawny frames, and yet Gemini tossed them around like they were nothing but rags. From where Celia knelt, I could see her twisting the makeshift tweezers, her face flushing from heat and apparent stress.

Gem's snarls increased and so did his volatile motions. Tears streamed down my face. "Celia, get it out!"

She sighed and removed the tweezers, watching in frustration as his skin sealed shut, and taking care to avoid Aric's gaze. "I'm sorry, but I'm trying to reach between the small space in his ribs."

"Should you break them again?" Liam suggested, to which I almost wigged out on him.

She brushed the perspiration from her crown with the back of her forearm, taking a moment to consider her options. "No. It would mean sawing a hole into his back."

I thought Emme would puke again. In truth, I wanted to. "Oh, goodness. *Why?*" Emme asked.

Celia pointed with her tweezers, careful not to touch him. "You see that mark?" I craned my neck to look and nodded along with the others. "Given the spot, and how far I'm having to dig, I think the bullet's lodged in his kidney."

"His *kidney?*" I rose slowly, but the moment my hands slipped from Gemini's shoulders, he hurtled Koda into the wall and Liam against our granite counter. The sheer force Gemini used to break free sent Celia soaring. She flipped off the table, landing in a deep crouch, her tigress eyes replacing her own.

Growls erupted from all the wolves present, rattling the windows. Gemini ignored them, along with the frantic shouts of his parents. He rose with his feet firmly planted on the floor, his glare trained directly on Aric.

My hands gripped my lover's waist. Although his human body remained, he was all wolf then. If it weren't for the control he managed, two humongous wolves would be hunting prey in our kitchen.

I splayed my hand across his chest, trying to keep him in place. "Baby, *stop.*" My head whipped behind me. "What's happening—why is he acting like this?" And why was he going after his Leader?

Aric met Gem with equal anger, biting out his words. "Rage

stirred from his torment have replaced his humanity. His wolves demand blood and vengeance for his suffering."

Shock shrilled my voice. "But you're his fucking alpha!"

"Which makes me the biggest threat here," Aric ground out, his eyes flashing with ire.

My insides shriveled inward as I realized what was happening. In the wild, wolves fought, often to death, to lead the pack as alpha. In his pain, Gemini wasn't thinking straight. If he were, he wouldn't be challenging Aric for a shot at top dog—or demanding someone pay for his suffering. That was bad, but considering Aric *was* alpha, he couldn't dismiss the challenge or appear subservient before his pack.

My hands pressed against Gemini's chest. "Gem, listen to me—"

I gasped when he pulled me into a protective clutch, his glare staying locked on Aric.

Aric prowled forward, readying to fight if that's what it took to control Gemini. "Don't make me do this," he warned.

Celia lurched forward, intercepting him. "Aric, *don't.*"

Aric froze, his vicious wolf snarling at Gem, who growled back with identical force. Celia glanced back at us, fear reaching her features, knowing our wolves were seconds from ripping each other apart. She lifted her hands and placed them over Aric's chest. "Aric, look at me," she whispered. "I need you to look at me, okay?"

Despite his anger, his attention left Gemini and focused on her as she whispered something I couldn't hear. The thing was, I couldn't keep looking at them. Not with Gem so out of his mind.

Again, he lurched forward, growling a warning at Liam and Koda when they advanced. "Get back," I hissed, surprising them and me, as I held Gem in place with just a squeeze of my arms.

I placed my cheek against his chest. I didn't know what

Celia was doing or saying. I only knew it was enough to keep Aric from attacking. He wrenched her behind him, shielding her with his body but failing to move as she continued to murmur almost silently, her eyes pleading with him to hear her words.

She was soothing her mate with her voice and touch. Maybe I needed to do the same. My lips passed along Gemini's skin. I spoke softly as I stroked his sweat-soaked back. "I get that you're pissed and get that you're hurting. But, baby, I need you to stay calm." I looked up, witnessing enough fury lurking behind his dark irises to startle me. "Tomo, please look at me," I begged.

I wasn't sure if he would, given his state. But he did, meeting my face with an expression so warm, my body melted against him. "You're my strength. You know you are. You have been since the day you walked into my life." I released a breath, not caring anymore who was listening. "I can't tell you how close I am to busting everything up. So, stay strong for me, so I can be strong for you." By then I was crying, but I couldn't seem to stop. "I love you, Tomo. *Please* . . . be the hero you've always been in my heart."

Everyone stilled, including me, fearful of what would happen next. Gemini might have been Aric's loyal friend, but my wolf seethed with unfathomable rage.

Aric's jaw set tight, his stare unflinching as he and Gem faced off once more.

The strain in the seconds that followed threatened to snap my skull clear off my shoulders. Aric wouldn't hurt me. And Gemini wouldn't risk hurting me to charge him. That didn't mean they wouldn't hurt each other.

My legs almost gave out from under me when Gemini responded by breaking eye contact with Aric to address Celia. "My apologies," he said, his tone stiff with pain and his beasts' remaining fury. "If you're still willing to help me, I'll return to the table."

"I'm still willing." Her attention skimmed briefly to Aric. "He didn't hurt me," she assured him.

"*Good,*" Aric growled in response. He looked to her, taking in the way that he held her against him, before releasing her slowly.

Celia tore away from him the second his hands slipped to his sides. She bent to lift the discarded tweezers, ignoring him once more. "Taran, come here. I need you to sterilize them."

Weres were immune to diseases and infections except those caused by cursed gold or magic. Celia knew as much, but old nursing habits die hard . . . or perhaps she needed a moment to collect herself. Anyone could see the effect Aric's presence and contact had had on her, despite her best efforts to remain calm. I pushed up on my toes and kissed Gem's chin, the gesture encouraging him to loosen his hold.

Once I was satisfied Gem wouldn't go wolf again, I walked to Celia and held open my palm, forming a crackling ball of blue and white flame. Celia spun the tweezers over them as Gem lowered himself across the table, his face scrunching with every movement. The holes in his back and chest had fully mended, but he favored the side where the bullet remained wedged in his damn kidney. It was all I could do not to lose it.

Celia removed the tweezers from my flame. The air swooshed around my trembling palm as I withdrew my power.

She kept her face dead on mine, but it was our sisters she spoke to. "Shayna, I need you to adjust the shape of the tweezers. Thin out the tips and add teeth, as many as you can manage. I also need a sharper and thinner scalpel, and more clamps so that you and Emme can hold the skin open from both sides. His skin and surrounding muscles are healing too fast and obstructing my view."

My full attention locked on Celia. She shook her head,

apologetically. She knew I was close to my breaking point. "Taran, I have to get this bullet out."

Emme practically fell over herself to gather more utensils for Shayna to transform. Shayna inched over and lifted the tweezers from Celia's grasp, her tone cautious when sparks of flame engulfed my hands. "She's only trying to help, T."

My eyes stung because clearly, I hadn't cried enough. "I'm not mad. I just . . . it's hard to see him like this. I don't know how much more I can take."

"I know," Celia said. "And I'm going to make it right. Just stay strong, okay?"

I tried to nod, but the motion seemed awkward. I shook my hands out, and their fire. As I watched, Shayna's magic manipulated the metal to roughen the ends, her concentration intense and her work detailed to create the fine yet jagged points.

I whirled away before she finished and lifted the chair that had toppled over. I placed it in front of Gemini and reached for his hand. His thumb brushed over my knuckles as he pushed up from the table and onto his forearms.

Currents of agony swirled along his irises as his dark almond eyes blinked back at me, yet it was my presence that drew his concern. He brushed his lips over my knuckles. "Don't be afraid. As long as you want me, I'll never leave you."

A sob broke through my chest as I buried my head against his shoulder. This was complete and pure torture. How had Celia survived when Aric was shot up with pure gold? I knew it had been agony for her—and that he'd been worse off—but I could barely keep it together. I clutched Gem tighter when he released another pained moan, praying I could get us through this.

The longer I waited, the more my emotions flared out of control, and the more it became clear just how much Celia had suffered and done for Aric in that one instance alone—when his body was riddled with gold—when he'd almost *died*. She'd fallen all over herself to care for him—clean his wounds, keep him calm, and watch over him despite her exhaustion.

He was her world, and because of it, she bit through her pain, shoved her needs aside, and saved him from the infection racking his body.

And he still left her.

Son of a bitch, he *still* left her. Was this my eventual fate, too? All these tears, all we'd been through, were they all for nothing?

Gemini's groans increased. But there was nothing anyone could do. We were waiting on Shayna to finish the tools Celia needed.

"Shhhh. Try to breathe," I said softly. I stroked his hair, wanting to distract him and wishing I could take away all his hurt. Yet even if I could, and no matter how it killed me to see him this way, I realized that like Aric, he could still dump me . . . no matter what he claimed.

I lifted my head when Aric placed a chair beside me and sat. "You, *incredible asshole,*" I told him.

Emme's gasp was the only sound heard in the sudden silence. Okay. I'll admit it. That was probably uncalled for.

Aric's frown relaxed as he seemed to realize what had triggered my reaction. Regret tightened his features and his attention drifted to Celia. Yeah. This idiot knew what I was thinking then.

Celia kept her chin lowered and placed her hand over Gem's shoulder, her voice shaky although it wasn't from fear. No, my girl was feeling something far worse. "I'm going to have to straddle your back to get into a good position. Are you okay with that?" She looked to me. "Both of you?"

"Do what you have to," Gem muttered. His hand continued to stroke mine.

I wiped a tear away and nodded. Koda and Liam edged

closer. Aric raised his hand, keeping them in place. "Don't. It's not necessary. As his mate, Taran alone can keep him calm."

Liam raised his brows. "She wasn't able to earlier. Gem lost it, even with her here."

"That was before," Aric said.

I knitted my brows. "Before what?"

Aric seemed to see right through me. "Before you finally accepted what you could do for him as his mate." He ignored the shock that struck me like a slap. "Whatever you do, don't let him go," he rumbled.

There was a lot that went unsaid in those words—for me, and for Celia. Aric felt guilt for leaving my sister. I knew that. Just like I knew he shared in her pain.

How could you break her heart? I wanted to ask. Yet I couldn't. Not then. Instead, I looked to the wolf who held mine in his grip. My hand squeezed Gemini's tighter as I draped my free arm around his neck. I kissed him then, sweeping my tongue over his. It was brief, but it packed a punch. A flicker of desire replaced the hurt shadowing his features, if only for a moment. "Ready?" I asked.

At his nod, Celia climbed on his back and reached for the scalpel. Blood spurted when she hit a vessel. "Hold the wound open," she urged my sisters. "I see it."

Gemini's spine bowed as Celia dug in like she was screwing in a bolt. I swear to Christ; had I been standing I would have crashed to the floor. I clutched him tighter, focusing on holding him close and trying to breathe, barely aware of Aric's small reassuring words.

Something dinged against the wall and Gem's body slumped. Around me the wolves swore. "It's out," Celia said, panting. "I got it."

19

Aric rose when Gemini pushed up on his forearms. I stood, too, albeit not as smoothly. Beads of sweat gathered around Gem's forehead, but as I watched, his skin resumed a healthier glow.

I just about keeled over when Gemini leapt onto the floor and carefully straightened. He wasn't one hundred percent—not by a long shot—but the results were astounding. The tension lifted from my back and neck. My wolf was going to be okay.

"You all right?" Aric asked him.

Gemini rubbed his forehead as he gathered me to him. "Tired, still sick, but my wolves are healing me." He paused. "I apologize about before."

Aric crossed his arms, tilting his chin slightly. They were besties, and both would risk their lives for each other. Yet times like this required Aric to assert his position as Leader. I understood. And I was grateful for his help.

But that didn't make their encounter any less scary.

He looked to me, his expression rigid. "Do we have your permission to conference in your family room?"

I nodded, holding tight to Gemini's hand as we led Aric out of the kitchen and into our large, open family room. He spoke quietly to Gemini, gathering the facts about what happened, and working out a plan to hunt the surviving Tribe *weres*. Liam and Koda took a seat on the couch opposite us. His parents took the loveseat, adding to the conversation when needed.

I remained tight-lipped, watching my sisters in the kitchen from where I sat. Shayna and Emme gathered around Celia when she peeled off her sweatshirt and tossed it in the trash. They didn't speak to her, knowing she was hurting having Aric so close. Her inner tigress had silenced her movements. I hadn't even noticed her leap from the table. Then again, I'd been close to hurling.

Shayna wrapped her spaghetti arms around her shoulders as Celia washed the blood caking her hands and wrists at the sink before stepping aside. Emme rubbed Celia's arm, yet it was as if neither had touched her. Celia concentrated fully on her task, working fast. Girlfriend was close to rubbing that first layer of skin clean off.

"Take the next few days to be with your family," Aric told Gemini, his tense voice drawing my attention. "I'll inform the Elders of what happened. If they require more information, I'll have them call you directly." He cocked his head in the direction of Gem's mother, his brows drawing tight. "You wish to say something, Mother Hamamatsu?"

"We ask for passage on to your Den and request use of your quarters."

"Our Den would be honored by your presence, and that of your mate," Aric responded. He rose and bowed before them. I take it the right way.

Gem's parents rose, too, exchanging bows. As Aric straightened, his attention drifted back to Celia, now only dressed in a tiny black tank that hugged her toned figure. I shouldn't have been surprised. He never could pry his eyes off her.

Celia finished drying her hands, well aware of the attention she was receiving. She folded the towel carefully and embraced my sisters. "Call me if you need me, okay?"

She crossed into the family room, staying so far away from Aric her ass almost brushed against the wall. "I'm glad you're safe," she said in our direction. "If you need me, let me know."

"Thank you, Celia," Gemini said quietly.

At her subtle nod, Liam and Koda murmured their good-byes, and Gem's parents bowed. Celia forced a small smile and attempted to hurry out.

Aric called to her, stalking forward. "Celia, wait."

His voice cemented her in place, but it was his clasp to her hand that hitched her breath and caused a quiver to rack along their forms. Aric closed his eyes and took an unsteady breath, followed by at least three more.

While he seemed to barely grip her, his hold welded them together and kept her in place. He opened his eyes, and Celia did, too. "Thank you for helping my brother," he said.

Her hand slipped from his. Again, all she could manage was a nod. It was like the rest of us had disappeared. They locked gazes, their shared misery bonding them and freezing time. "I don't mean to force you from your home," he said softly. "I apologize for my presence."

The sadness dulling her beautiful face was as tangible as my clasp to Gem's hand. "It's fine. I have to get back."

Aric's jaw tightened. "To *him*," he responded with a growl.

Celia slapped her hands against her sides. "What do you expect, Aric? We both have new lives to return to."

She could have said more, but she held back. She didn't want to hurt him.

"I wish things could be different," he admitted.

It was at that moment that I caught the barest hint of his vulnerability—the frustration, the anger, yeah, those were way more obvious. But I think it was his vulnerability that chinked

Celia's armor and glistened her eyes with tears. "I don't see how."

Neither did Aric. "Don't go back to him," was his sole response.

It was then Celia's anger flared. "Don't make this about Misha. And don't tell me what to do. Your opinion no longer mattered the day you walked away."

Aric's fists clenched and his head lowered when she crossed the threshold and shut the door behind her. Everyone there regarded him with sympathy, as if they could sense every sliver of his regret and heartbreak.

Everyone had always been nicer than me. "It's taking all I have not to knock you out right now," I told him. Gemini was at my heels as I stormed toward Aric. "How can you just let her go?"

Aric's chest rose and fell with each ragged breath, but he wouldn't answer.

"Answer me," I demanded. I pointed to the door even though Celia was probably long gone by now. "She gave you everything, Aric—*everything*. And how did you repay her? By walking away and into the arms of a total psycho."

"Taran—" he began.

I cut him off. "Don't tell me you have no choice. Don't tell me about your sense of duty. Just tell me how after all she did for you, and after how hard she loved you, you could just turn your back on her." Tears born of resentment and honesty blurred my vision. "She offered you her heart, Aric . . ."

The sniffles behind me told me I didn't cry alone. I didn't have to turn around to know Shayna' and Emme's eyes were pooling with tears.

My mouth opened, ready to say more. But as I watched him, all thoughts and words spun inside my head, making me dizzy.

Love wasn't beautiful; it wasn't pure. Love was brutal. Never had a word existed that could be so cherished and hated from one breath to the next.

I barely sensed Emme's gentle caress against my skin, and Gemini's tightening hold. The only thing I felt was sick and empty then. I pinched the bridge of my nose, trying to keep from crying as I realized nothing anyone said would send Aric charging after Celia, and that without him, my sister would spend her life alone, mourning what once was, and would never be again.

Numbness and something else claimed Aric. For all his strength and power, he seemed so defeated. He faced the Hamamatsus and bowed. "I'll wait outside until you're ready." He straightened slowly, then turned on his heel and stalked out the door.

One by one, everyone dispersed, leaving Gem and me alone with his parents. The four of us stood there, the events of the last few days appearing to encase us in lead. We'd taken on demons, vamps, and *weres*, and almost died. We'd bled, had the shit knocked out of us, and Gem had had his heart blown out and bullets dug from his skin.

That moment between me and Aric had been one of many, nothing compared to the feel of Gemini's lifeless form in my arms. But it was the knockout punch, and maybe something more.

I did a double take when I realized Momma and Pop were eying me with the same "we just sucked on rotten lemons" scowls. I guessed that yelling at a revered pureblood probably topped their Taran Sucks list.

"You're not what we expected, Taran Wird," Pop said.

I managed a smirk. "Yeah. I kinda figured."

His stare bounced to Gemini before landing back on me. "But you truly are Tomo's mate."

I stiffened my spine, knowing he was right, and fully accepting the meaning of that long dreaded word.

The quiet lengthened between us. Just when I thought I should say something more, Gemini's parents bowed.

We returned the gesture in silence. Slowly, the elderly duo made their way to the front door. I thought the night would end like that, quiet with only our breaths, until Momma paused and glanced back, meeting my face directly with hers. "Thank you," she said.

I raised my brows. *For swearing, for throwing you off a mountain, for singeing your fur and making you bald?* As it was, her hair still hadn't grown back. "Pardon?" I managed.

Her voice was absolute. "For loving our son," she said.

I gaped at the closed door even long after she shut it behind her. That woman would likely never call me to go shopping, or to have lunch, or be the mother I'd missed, and longed for. She didn't approve of me; she didn't like my clothes, the way I talked, or possibly even the way I walked.

But she knew I loved her son. Out of everything she'd witnessed and the multiple times I'd screwed up, somehow, I managed to show her what Gemini meant to me.

I crossed my arms and shook my head. At least I'd gotten something right.

I leaned heavily on Gem when his arms gathered me to him. "Do you want to eat?" I asked him. "You must be famished."

"Later. What I need now is rest, love."

I groaned. There was that "L" word again. Of all the four-letter words I knew, it was the one capable of causing the most pain. Celia and Aric had more than proven it.

Gem's palm pressed against my back as he led me into our room. "What are you thinking robout?" he asked.

He lowered himself to the edge of the bed and clutched my hands as he waited for me to answer. "Believe it or not, Aric and Celia," I told him.

"I recognize your need to protect your sister. But considering all we endured, I find your preoccupation with them odd." He adjusted his hold. "Why did their interaction upset you so much? It was as if you were hurting for them."

I wasn't sure how to explain what I felt. He was right; I did hurt for them. But it wasn't as simple as that. The other piece of the Taran puzzle . . . well, that stirred something entirely different. "They loved each other."

He considered me as he played with my hands. It was then I could see just how tired he was. "They still do," he admitted.

Tears swirled my vision. "Yeah. And that's what makes this so wrong. Everything my sister did, and everything she felt, didn't matter. Gem, she's risked her *life* for him—"

"Just as he has for her, and just as he would even now that they're apart."

He had to go and say that. But I wasn't done. My voice shook. "He made her soul bleed."

"And bled his own out in the process."

I tried to settle—and not cry like those women on TV who wailed over the tiniest thing that went wrong. I took a few breaths, but of course it didn't work. My shoulders shook for how hard I cried then. "But he walked away," I insisted once again. "All this suffering—all his willingness to lay down his life for someone he abandoned, for everything Celia supposedly means to him—it's not enough. They're not together, and will never be together, no matter how hard they love each other."

Gemini gathered me onto his lap, watching me intently. "What was the point of all of it?" I asked him. "Why did they even bother?"

He pushed my hair away from my face. "We're not really talking about Aric and Celia, are we?"

I tensed against him. "Yes, we are."

I didn't have to see him then to know he was smiling. He pressed a kiss onto the side of my face and chuckled. "You may use their names, and your words may have merit. But I think your worry and pain surpass their situation and reflect onto ours."

I opened my mouth, ready to argue, but shut it instead and muttered a curse. Sometimes it didn't pay to have a smart boyfriend. If he were dumb and sexy, this thing could be a lot easier and way more fun.

Gemini kneaded my hip. "They hurt, and they're apart, that's true. But if they could somehow relive their time together, I know that they would."

His voice lowered to a rumble. "There are no guarantees in life, Taran. But Aric and Celia have demonstrated that the love they share will burn through eternity."

"And so will their misery."

"Perhaps. But when adoration runs so deep, so does its torment."

"That's another one of those Zen things you people throw around, isn't it?"

This time, he did chuckle. "No. That one was all me."

I sighed, allowing my head to fall against his shoulder. Although it was caked with God knows what, he swept his lips over my brow, speaking barely above a whisper. "Our life together hasn't been perfect. We've argued and hurt each other more times than I wish. I'd like to say it won't happen again, but given—"

"My attitude, short fuse, rage?" I offered.

He drew me closer. "I meant to say that given the state of our world, our troubles are far from past us." He cupped my face and lifted it so I'd meet his gaze, the look in his eyes as patient as his smile. "But all things aside, I need you to believe that I would rather endure the hardships that await us than to never have known you. I love you, Taran."

Yeah. Me too, baby.

I wiped the tears that followed before slipping from his lap. His dark eyes sizzled as I yanked the remains of my dress over my head. I rolled my shoulders following the toss of my bra (the girls needed to breathe, after all) and kept my gaze locked on his as I peeled off my panties. I held tight to his jaw when I straddled him and lowered my lips to meet his hungry mouth.

Gem flipped me onto my back, stripping out of his sweat-pants, his bare skin warm and ready to push inside of mine.

This wasn't about sex. Not this time.

It was simply my turn to be claimed.

SNEAK PEEK . . .

Read on for an excerpt from
Of Flame and Light
by Cecy Robson

20
____

You know it's going to be a bad day when you wake up in the morning and the first word out of your mouth is "fuck."

My right arm—or should I say my *new* arm generated after my real one was chewed off by a psycho werewolf (no, this isn't a joke) —buzzes me awake. That's right, *buzzes*.

I do my best to hide my limb. Not just because it's as white as alabaster. Or because of the fluorescent blue veins that run its length. But because it's doing things I can't control, like, interfering with my magic, glowing like a light saber, and now, making noise.

I lift my head, half-asleep, wondering how a wasp nest found its way beneath my pillow, but too exhausted to run away screaming, *yet*. If you were familiar with my life and world, you'd understand pissed off wasps in my bed wouldn't be the craziest or scariest thing that's ever happened to me.

My eyes narrow at the quivering pillow as my haze clears. Maybe I'm tired, or maybe it's because I'm bitter as all hell, but I can't help thinking that the arm *and* the pillow are laughing at me. I pull my glowing and buzzing arm from beneath the fluffy white pillow and swear.

"Really? *Really*?" I ask it. "What's next, singing and origami?"

Apparently, my incandescent light saber arm isn't a fan of sarcasm and proceeds to flicker on and off like a twisted strobe light. I shake it hard and smack it against the mattress, for all the good it does. "Knock it off," I tell it.

It's not that I think it listens, or that I manage to control it. There's simply no controlling this thing, but somehow the glowing recedes and so does the noise, and my arm resumes its "normal" death-like tone.

It quiets, no longer casting light. I should be thankful, right? I should be happy, true?

Oh, I wish.

The color is startling and contrasts horrifically against my deep olive skin. But its eerie tone and its unpredictability aren't the only things that trouble me. There's something wrong with this limb. It doesn't belong on me. And in a way, it doesn't belong in this world.

Maybe, like me, it's something that wasn't supposed to be.

I sigh and clutch it against me. It feels like my old arm, the skin soft and smooth. It moves like my old arm. I'm not limited with either fine or gross motor skills. But it's not . . . *human*.

When I lost my real arm, the Squaw Valley Pack Omega, created this new one using ancient werewolf magic. If I were a *were*, I think things would have been fine, peachy-keen, and all that good stuff. But I'm not a *were*, or human, or witch, or vampire, or anything. Not even a little bit.

My sisters and I may look human, but nothing like us have ever existed on earth. And, because of it, Earth's ancient magic seems to really resent helping a weird girl like me.

I used to wield fire and lightning with ease and catch glimpses of the future. I used to be a badass. I'm no longer a badass, and the only things I catch now are odd glances cast my way.

"Are you the punishment for my sins?" I ask my arm.

I don't expect it to answer, but it does. Sputtering light and buzzing before abruptly ceasing its response and sinking into the mattress.

To anyone watching, this whole thing might be funny. To me . . . nothing's been funny in a long time.

For a moment, I simply stare at it. There's a part of me that wants to cry, wondering what it will start doing next. But I've already cried too long and hard for what it has cost me.

Or should I say, *who* it cost me.

I scan the room. Nothing of Gemini remains. Not his clothes, not our pictures together. I even deleted and blocked his number. For all my arm disgusts me, I never expected it to disgust him more. After all, this was the werewolf who claimed me as his mate. The same male who swore he'd love only me forever.

I suppose forever only counts so long as I didn't change, so long as I remained perfect in his eyes. But I never claimed to be perfect, even if many believed I'd looked the part.

My arm flickers and *zings*, the electrified charge is strong enough to startle me and slap any remnants of sleep away. Yeah. No way am I perfect. Not by a long shot, especially with this thing constantly mocking me and reminding me of every- thing wrong in my life.

A sharp rap to the door has me glancing toward my right. "Taran?" my perky sister Shayna calls. "I heard your alarm clock go off. Want some breakfast?"

I lift the bane of my existence and sigh. Alarm clock? I suppose that's one word for it.

"T?" Shayna presses. "I'm making waffles."

She semi-sings her last few words which is a very "Shayna" thing to do.

"I'll be right out," I answer.

"Cool!" she responds. "I have plenty."

It's not that I want to eat. It's that I know how worried my sisters are about me. So, I sit with them when I can, and plaster on a smile when I need to, but even that's burdensome, which sucks. I don't want my time with my sisters to be a chore. I love them. But I've learned some things can't be helped.

My arm fires with its haunting glow. Case in point.

With a groan, I slip out of bed, pulling on a fresh pair of panties and a bra before heading to my bathroom to clean up. After a few swipes of mascara and some lipstick, I yank on a form-fitting red dress and shove my feet into a pair of platform pumps, doing my best to strut and not collapse back in bed. Yet even though I'm almost to the door, there's one more thing I need. Most women won't leave their homes without their cell phones. I can't leave my room without my elbow-length gloves. It helps me hide the ugly appendage and the light show that accompanies it.

But now that my arm's buzzing . . .

I pause with my hand on the doorknob. What am I going to do about this thing?

I take a breath and wrench open the door, tugging on my gloves as I walk down the hall and into our large kitchen. Shayna abandons the waffle iron when she sees me and skips forward, her ponytail bouncing behind her.

She throws her arms around me like it's been months, not hours, since she's seen me. "Hey, T!" she tells me brightly.

I pat her back, wishing I could hug her for real. But real hugs lead to my very real tears, and I can't keep doing this to my family. "Hey, princess. Wow, everything smells great."

It's the truth, yet my comment sounds phony and forced, even to me.

Her arms fall away slowly. Although she keeps her grin, I

sense the worry behind it, as well as her fear. "You look hot," she tells me, punching my good arm affectionately.

No. I look acceptable. I used to spend over an hour styling my dark wavy hair and applying my makeup. Now, I do enough so I don't resign myself to sweats, watching made for TV movies, and stuffing my face with potato chips.

"Thanks," I manage with yet another forced grin. I make a show of taking in all the breakfast foods, including the freshly baked muffins. "Yum. Do you need help setting the table or anything?"

"No. It's all good."

She says nothing more which is unusual for Shayna. Either she's waiting for me to speak or she's debating what to say. I can't take another pity party, so I lift a pan filled with eggs and plate stacked with waffles and bring them to the table. "Where's your puppy?" I ask. Or in other words, where's your gigantic scary werewolf husband, Koda?

"Oh, he already ate and left. He's doing more at the Den since Celia's been needing more ah, time with Aric."

Okay, now I really grin, and so does she. Time with Aric is a mild way to describe what Celia desires from her husband.

Our youngest sister Emme walks out of the laundry room blushing, which tells me she's heard us discussing Celia. Shayna's grin quickly turns into a laugh. Emme's shyness has that effect on her.

Emme clears her throat, but not her obvious discomfort. Where Shayna has dark straight hair, Emme has soft blonde waves and fair skin that reddens the longer we take her in.

"Emme," I offer. "What's the big deal? So, what if Celia's banging Aric like the lead drummer at a Fourth of July parade. They're married. It happens."

Emme holds up her hand. "Taran, please let's keep their private life private."

I reach for a glass of freshly squeezed juice. "I would if they weren't so damn loud. I swear, I thought the walls were going to come down around midnight when they—"

"Taran . . ." Emme whimpers, shaking her hands like she can't stand to hear another word.

Emme's always been so sweet and angelic. Me? Not at all. "Hey, do you suppose Celia's more flexible now, given how Aric knocked her up? As in ankles behind the head kind of flexible—"

Emme lifts a muffin with her *force* and sends it soaring. I catch it just before it rams me in the mouth. "Eat," she insists. "Just eat."

In other words, for once in your life, shut your inappropriate trap.

Shayna takes a seat beside me, laughing her skinny ass off. Emme sits, too, in time for Celia to stagger down the back steps.

Good God. Celia's long curly hair is tousled from lack of sleep and the insane amount of sex she's had. And her eyes are glazed with a hunger that warns me not to get too close. "Is there bacon? Please tell me there's bacon," she growls as if crazed.

Her entire face beams when Emme levitates a plateful of bacon and lowers it in front of an empty seat. Like a woman possessed, Celia sits and rams about four pieces in her mouth at once. The rest of us watch her in stunned silence as she chomps them down and reaches for another few slices. She freezes when she realizes we're all gaping at her. "Sorry. Would you like some?"

Her tigress eyes replace her human ones, making it clear she's only trying to be polite. And that only an idiot would get between her and her breakfast.

"No, nope, uh-uh," the three of us answer at once.

This seems to settle her inner beast enough so Celia's human eyes once more blink back at us. I pour her a glass of juice, while Emme and Shayna carefully place plates stacked with food closer to her reach. What can I say, we don't want to be eaten.

"Are you all right?" Emme asks her quietly.

Celia slows her frantic munching. "I don't know," she admits, her husky voice trickling with concern. She lifts her T-shirt and shows us her tiny belly. "The baby's not growing."

We've noticed that, too. Her pregnancy had been unexpected, given she was incapable of bearing children. But within two weeks of finding out she and Aric had conceived, her baby bump had appeared and was visible through her wedding gown.

That was two months ago. And now, despite how this baby has been prophesized to rid the world of evil, we're all pretty much freaking out that he or she isn't growing.

"But your body's changing," I insist. I don't exactly ooze optimism. In fact, I'm a *the sky is falling and the earth is swallowing us whole* kind of gal. But Celia doesn't need to hear what's wrong. My girl needs hope and that's what I give her. I point to her chest. "If your hooters don't scream 'I'm knocked up', I don't know what does."

She glances at her girls and then back at me, the tension in her shoulders lifting slightly. "They are a lot bigger," she agrees quietly. She gathers her thoughts, appearing to want to say more despite her obvious hesitation. "And my body does feel like it's becoming something more. Maybe not outwardly, but I can feel the difference inside of me."

"What are you feeling, Ceel?" Shayna asks. "Is your magic changing?"

Celia nods. "The magic that helped me get pregnant seems to complement mine. But my hormones are out of control." Her cheeks flush and she lowers her voice. "Poor Aric. I can't stop having sex with him. It's like every time I see him, I pounce."

Aric bounds down the steps as if called, his eyes glassy from lack of sleep and his five o'clock shadow now a full-out beard thanks to his preference to satisfy Celia's needs rather than shave. His face lights up when he sees Celia, kind of like she did at the sight of bacon.

"Yeah, poor bastard," I mutter.

"Hey, beautiful," he says to Celia, bending to kiss her lips.

She smiles against his mouth. "Hey, wolf," she answers, stroking his beard lightly.

Emme inches away when Celia's stare suggests the need for something more than breakfast. Aric, being Aric, returns that look with equal force. I start to laugh, not because of Celia and Aric, but because of Emme's response. She's glancing around at the food like she knows it's going to end up splattered across Celia's and Aric's soon-to-be naked bodies.

My laugh lodges in my throat when my right arm jerks as if shocked. Shayna lowers her fork. "You okay, T?" she asks.

I shove my arm under the table. "Fine," I say. I reach for glass of juice with my opposite hand, trying to stay calm. Celia and Emme didn't notice my twitch, and I don't think Aric did either, but something about me lures his attention away from Celia.

He cocks his head, his nose flaring as if his alpha wolf has latched onto something. "Taran, what's wrong?" he asks.

Celia's and Emme's attention drifts my way. Shayna rises, fear crinkling her brow.

"I'm tired," I say dismissively, feeling my pulse start to race. I push my chair out. "I should head back to bed. I didn't sleep much—"

All at once, and without warning, pain burns its way across my affected limb, curling me forward in agony. My arm whips out, sending the table and all its contents soaring with freakish speed. Plates shatter on the floor as the table imbeds, with a loud bang, *into* the wall, directly above where Celia sat seconds before.

I lift my head as the burn recedes, searching for her,

panicked I harmed her. Tears of relief and residual pain slide down my face when I see Aric lower her to floor and far away from me. She and our sisters stare back at me stunned. But Aric? Holy shit, he's *pissed*.

"Taran, what are you doing?" he growls.

I shake my head, knowing he's angry I almost hurt Celia. "I'm not doing anything . . ."

The burn returns and so does its torment. This time, I can't bite back my screams. I stumble forward. Aric races to me. I don't see him. I only feel his body and hear the crunch of bone when my arm flails and connects with his jaw.

He crashes against the granite counter with a grunt as my arm jerks wildly and the burn increases tenfold.

My vision fades in and out and my body thrashes, the erratic movements of my limb throwing me against the wall. I collapse, my arm still beating itself against the floor with enough force to splinter and punch through the wood. I'm not thinking. I can't. Everything hurts.

No. Everything *burns*.

"Cut it off!" I scream.

Shayna reaches for a knife, elongating it with her power and manipulating it into a deadly sword. She lifts the blade above my spastic arm, her expression torn. By now I'm sobbing, and all but clawing at my face.

"*Please*," I beg her. "Cut it off!"

"I can't," Shayna chokes out. "I can't do this."

"Pin it," Celia yells. "Pin it to the floor!"

With a flick of her wrists Shayna changes the sword's position and brings the point down toward my raging hand. I barely feel the prick before the room erupts in a ghostly light and Shayna goes flying.

Emme screams as Shayna collides into the far wall. Aric and Celia are scrambling forward, but all thoughts are lost in my torture. I'm retching with how hard I'm crying and from the anguish crawling from my arm and into my chest.

Just as the burn reaches my heart and I begin to lose consciousness, a pale yellow light surrounds me. Slowly, very slowly, the heat charring my insides is replaced with a soothing chill I welcome like a draw of fresh air.

My body shudders as the coolness spreads like a cascade of water from a gentle spring. My pain eases and my cries dwindle. It takes a long time for the ache to lessen, and even longer for my vision to clear. But eventually it does.

Not that I like what I see.

Blood cakes the side of Shayna's face. She winces as the bone along her eye socket pops out and the cut above her eyebrow knits close. Bile churns my gut. If Koda hadn'tpassed her a portion of his werewolf essence, I would have killed her. There's no doubt. based on the amount of blood coating her skin, and what her body had to do to heal her indented skull.

I cover my mouth. "Oh, my God," I gasp.

"It's okay, T," she says, as if I can't see the pain tightening her small pixie face. "It's okay."

No. Not at all, sweetie.

Aric leans forward. Being a werewolf and of pure blood, his inner beast had healed him faster than Shayna. That didn't mean I hadn't made rubble out of his jaw or that I hadn't hurt him.

Or that I won't do it again.

I had no control over my arm. None. Nor do I believe I have it now.

Aric realizes as much. I don't miss how he keeps Celia behind him, appearing to shield her and their child from whatever I'll unleash next.

"What happened?" he asks, his voice riddled with anger, and maybe something more.

"I don't know," I respond, my voice trembling and my body strangely weak. "I felt pain and it-it went wild."

"Your arm?" It's a question, but he's not really asking.

I nod as Emme's healing light recedes and her hands withdraw from my shoulders. Her face is unusually pale. She swallows hard, struggling to speak. "It's her fire," she says, barely above a whisper. She looks at Aric. "It's eating her alive . . .

Cecy Robson is an international and multi-award winning author of over twenty-character driven novels. As a registered nurse of more than seventeen years, Cecy spends her free time creating magical worlds, heart-stopping romance, and young adult adventure. After receiving two RITA® nominations and winning the Maggie Award of Excellence, you can still find Cecy laughing, crying, and cheering on her characters as she pens her next story.

Visit Cecy online at cecyrobson.com

www.ingramcontent.com/pod-product-compliance
Lightning Source LLC
Chambersburg PA
CBHW050530190726

48284CB00003B/1010

* 9 7 8 1 9 4 7 3 3 0 2 8 3 *